PAID A PRETTY PENNY

James A.S. Ivan

ISBN: 978-0-6455776-0-0 (Paperback)
ISBN: 978-0-6455776-4-8 (Hardcover)
ISBN: 978-0-6455776-5-5 (eBook)

Any references to historical events, real people, or real places are used fictitiously. Names, characters, and places are products of the author's imagination.

First printing edition 2022.

Cover design by Andrew Cockroft and Matt Carr.
Book design by Andrew Cockroft.

https://www.jamesivan.com/
james@jamesivan.com

http://mattconcepts.com/

For Sophia, Isabella, and Chelsea

Also for Larry.
(I don't know Larry. But he probably deserves it.)

Table of Contents

Episode I. Personification of Payment

"I'm bored," Hana exclaimed suddenly and dramatically. She slouched back into the passenger chair behind the flight deck.

"Why don't you do something?" Aron asked without looking up from the console he was working on.

"I don't want to do something by myself."

Aron turned around quickly to check further back into the ship.

"Marc is still awake – which I wouldn't advise given we're arriving in 6 hours, and he needs to sleep before then. But since he's not going to sleep anyway, you could do something with him."

Hana thought about this for a second. "No, I don't want to do something with Marc. His idea of a fun activity is beating people at Hehed Party."

"Well, I'm busy, and he's the only other person on the ship," Aron pointed out.

"I know. It's maggoty," she said with a sigh. "What are you doing, anyway?"

"Trying to configure the new radio. Can't dock at Tungol if we can't talk to them."

"We can't talk to them anyway. None of us knows how to speak Tungolese."

"They have interpreters," Aron pointed out.

"Who's flying this thing if you're mucking about with the radio?" She asked suddenly, sitting up straight.

Aron waved one hand dismissively while working with the other. "We're in a steady flight. What could go wrong?"

"A lot of things! You'd be very quick to tell one of us off if we were doing something else."

"Yeah, well, it's my ship," he said with a smile. "You can take the controls if you like."

"Nah."

She sighed again; it was something to do that wasn't working. She stood up, slowly paced the length of the galley, and then made her way back to the front.

"How long are we going to stay there?" Hana asked. She leaned in over Aron's shoulder.

"An hour, at most," Aron replied.

"So I'm going to sleep right through it?"

"Well, from what I hear, you won't be missing much. Tungol is a bit backward."

"Yeah, but you can buy all sorts of things that are illegal in most places!"

"We've got no time for shopping. We're just unloading, loading, and then moving on," Aron said. "Besides, you're not bringing anything on my ship that will get me into trouble."

"Can't we at least hang around so I have a chance to get off the ship?" Hana pleaded.

"No time. We're stopping this long in the first place because the buyer wants to meet in person, for some reason." Aron rolled his eyes. "But we'll be stopping on Beadful for a full day at least. You can do what you like there."

"Oh! Can we go to —" Hana started, but Aron interrupted her.

"No! Well, you can if you want. It's a bit too expensive for me at the moment."

"Typical. We never do anything fun." Hana pouted.

"Yeah, well, to do fun stuff, you need money. To get money, you need to work."

"We work so much we don't have time to do fun stuff!"

"Yep," Aron said with a sigh.

"And I'm bored," Hana said emphatically. She stalked off to find food.

"Aren't we all?" Aron whispered to himself.

— — — — —

Six hours later, Aron was banging on Marc's bunk.

"Oi! Get up."

Marc jolted. He groaned and then rolled over.

"Are we docking soon?" He asked sleepily.

"No. We've docked. Thanks a lot for your help," Aron said with some annoyance in his voice.

Marc wearily rolled himself out of his bed.

"You docked by yourself?"

"Yes. I'm going to find our buyer. You stay here and get the stuff ready."

"I'm not staying here. I'm going to get some fireworks or something," Marc said. He stretched his arms high. Then he started digging around in his locker for something to wear.

"Fine. Just make sure the stuff is ready to unload when the buyer arrives. And make sure you're up in time for your shift in the future. I shouldn't have to keep waking you up."

"What is this, the navy?"

"You should probably be thankful I'm not a naval commanding officer."

"Ok, Captain! I'll be sure to be up at 14 bells, boots shined by 15 bells, and ready for duty at 16 bells."

"I'm serious. I don't like doing longer shifts because you don't set yourself an alarm."

"Whatever," Marc said, sitting down on the unused bunk to don his socks.

"Just... make sure the cargo is ready *before* you go on your shopping spree. And, F.Y.I., the bell system only goes up to eight. They just repeat it six times."

"Aye, aye, sir!" Marc saluted.

— — — — —

Tungol's Central Spaceport floated high above the planet, tethered to the ground below by the thin threads of five space elevators and supported by a solitary orbital ring. A central ring structure with docking terminals on its internal surfaces was at its core. Surrounding this was a very inconsistent set of extensions containing markets and commercial space. It looked like the results of years of uncontrolled development, but it was all relatively new. Tungol had only opened up to outside trade fifty years prior. This spaceport had only been built in the last ten years to replace the already overloaded original, which was still in use a few thousand kilometres along the orbital ring.

The planet itself was known for its short people and its steeped traditions. It had a stringent class system – not that you'd be aware walking around the spaceport. Everyone there shared only one purpose: to move products on or off the planet. The people working there were well prepared for dealing with outsiders; there were very few opportunities for someone to cross a social boundary. An outside trader wasn't expected to know the rituals. Third parties would handle all of those on the trader's behalf before they even arrived.

Despite all of this preparation, Aron found himself wandering around the spaceport's most extensive market, lost and needing directions. He had expected to be met by someone who would help him find his way. But unbeknownst to him, that person had come down ill on the way and had returned home. Having already wasted time waiting, Aron did not feel like wasting more time trying to fumble his way through the poorly translated directions. He wandered in what he hoped was the correct direction, stopping the occasional person and attempting to ask for directions. His requests were met with blank stare after blank stare. Finally, after at least a dozen false starts, he found someone willing to help.

"Gralu."

"Gralu," the man said as he walked passed.

"Hello. Do you speak English?" Aron asked, matching the man's pace.

"Yas. I spaik Englis," the man said, looking up at the tall stranger with interest.

"Finally!" Aron gushed. "I need help finding my way."

Aron showed him the note with the address that had so far proved unhelpful.

"I can halp. Bery close. I take you dar."

"Thank you," Aron replied enthusiastically. "My name is Aron."

"I am Petror."

At the man's beckoning, Aron followed him through the crowd. This was easier than it might sound, despite the surrounding people being tightly packed. The people of Tungol were much shorter than humans, but Petror, at 135cm, was amongst the taller ones. So it was easy to keep Petror within sight.

"Why you here?" Petror asked once they were out of the marketplace and clear of the noise.

"Pardon?"

"Why you cam to here? What you do here?"

"I'm here to sell some stuff. I have a buyer lined up at that address."

"What you sall?" Petror asked.

"M.R.S. chips," Aron responded.

"Vah! Dey sall bery aisy now. Gat good price!"

"I know."

— — — — —

After heading through a marketplace, their path took them down a comparatively sizeable road. About halfway down this road, Petror led Aron diagonally across a glass-domed park. The park was clearly intended to provide some relief from the monotony of corridors and enclosed roofs. But this park was littered with garbage. And while the trees seemed ok, the grass was withered and patchy. They headed down a much narrower road leading away from the park bounded by a neat row of offices with glass and stone facades. Their destination was not far down this road.

Aron was a bit apprehensive when he saw the size of the door. He wasn't a tall man (where he came from), but this door was tiny. Fortunately, the inside would prove more adequately proportioned: just high enough that he could walk with his hair only just brushing the ceiling.

Aron's new friend proved very helpful in making his introductions when the door was answered. Petror introduced both Aron and his purpose and proceeded to interpret everything either party said.

His client was impressed, commenting on the professionalism of bringing an interpreter instead of conducting the transaction by simply following the paperwork form. Aron remembered something he had read about Tungolese culture and deflected the compliment.

They were ushered into a very well-appointed inner office where the client walked through the main terms of the deal. Everything was going very well, right up to the point where the payment method needed to be discussed.

Petror suddenly stopped interpreting, and he and the client seemed to be having an intense conversation. Aron tried to ask what was being said, but Petror wasn't paying attention.

Before he knew it, Aron and Petror were being escorted out to the street.

"What did you say to him?" Aron asked, exasperated.

"He offar you ¤18,000. Too, too little!" Petror exclaimed.

"No, that's a fair transportation payment."

"Uh? Vah! I tought dat is salling price. I sorry!"

Aron screwed up his face; he felt a bit like screaming. But he composed himself. That attitude wasn't helpful: he didn't have time to panic.

"I need to look for new buyers. I just need to find someone else, and all will be ok," he assured himself.

"I halp you!"

Aron was torn. On the one hand, he didn't know this spaceport. It could take ages to find a new buyer. And that would be made exceedingly complicated by the language barrier. On the other hand, Petror had just ruined a good deal.

"Alright," Aron said. "But let me do the negotiations."

"Vah! Yas, yas."

— — — — —

It took an hour and a half, but they finally found a buyer who would take most of Aron's M.R.S. shipment for a reasonable price. Aron and the other buyer organised the payment and a pickup time.

Petror generously agreed to buy the last of Aron's supply from him and sell it on himself. Getting payment from Petror would require heading back to his place of business. But first, Aron needed to let Marc know what was going on. Since he didn't have a phone which would work on Tungol, he headed back to his ship with Petror tagging along. Petror phoned an assistant to meet them there and organise transport for the crates.

"What took you so long?" Marc asked.

"It's a long story."

"Did you get lost? Is this the guy?" Marc asked.

"Not exactly," Aron replied.

"What do you mean?"

"Deal fell through. Miscommunication."

"What? How?" Marc asked, surprised.

Aron sighed. "Doesn't matter now. I've sold the goods on. We've got two buyers. This is Petror. He'll be taking two hundred minicrates. Another group will be along soon to collect the rest. Hopefully, they'll have collected all their goods before the next load of containers arrives."

"Whatever. So long as we're not taking it home."

— — — — —

Petror's assistant soon arrived. Aron thought he must be a human. He was shorter than Aron (who is not tall) but much too tall to be Tungolese. Aron wasn't sure the assistant understood English, though. Aron attempted to introduce himself and then explain something to him, but all he got in reply was a blank stare.

Aron thought it was odd that Petror spoke English while the human who worked for him didn't. Eventually, Petror gave the assistant the explanation, and things started moving.

While Marc and Petror's unnamed assistant organised the transport of the goods by way of a makeshift sign language, Petror and Aron headed back to Petror's place of business to arrange payment. Petror's shop was only a few streets away, located at the corner of a large paved square with a flat glass roof.

Petror stopped Aron at the front door. "Listan, I sorry about broke deal. I must gibe you someting. It no good for me. Meybe good for you. Cober some your loss."

"You don't need to give me anything."

"No! I mast! I mast!" Petror said forcefully, shaking his head for emphasis. "I broke deal. I mast gibe you someting."

"Ok, if you insist."

Petror opened the door to his shop and led him inside. He immediately yelled something Aron didn't understand to a human girl who had been working behind the counter. After a very brief discussion (in which she barely spoke), the girl put down the books she had been working on and disappeared into the back room.

"I habe two. One, uh ... one both. But I gat no more of dam. So I gibe dis one to you," Petror said. He handed him a tiny device with a small screen and a set of buttons. Both of these showed writing in a script Aron wrongly assumed was the local language.

"Thank you. But I —"

"Dis, uh, buttans. Prass numbar like dis abery day."

Petror demonstrated entering a number and then made Aron repeat it until Petror was sure that Aron would remember it.

Aron wasn't sure what this device was nor why it would be so useful to him. Still, he pretended to be grateful, and then they settled down to organise the monetary payment.

They hadn't agreed on a price before this. But Petror was very generous with the price he offered. Aron was starting to feel optimistic about this trip – even if it was still not quite as profitable as it was supposed to have been.

"Stay. I go gat for you," Petror said once the business had been taken care of.

Petror disappeared into the back room and reappeared in a moment with the girl. He specifically drew Aron's attention to her. She had changed her clothes.

Before leaving, she was wearing smart business attire, a clean-pressed blouse and pants combination with a jacket and polished shoes. What she wore now was a ragged and very worn knee-length dress. It showed signs of having once been half-blue, half-white. But the blue was mostly gone, and the white was overtaken by grime. It had been made of thick material, but there were tears and holes – some in unwelcome places and which had been crudely patched or stitched closed. She had no shoes, socks, or jacket. Even her hair was loose where previously it had been tied. Aron guessed that maybe she had some messy tasks to complete. But why was Petror so keen for Aron to see her? To make sure Aron knew he had a human employee?

Petror brought her over. He stood the girl next to Aron and then smiled at her.

"Vah! One ting more," he said, holding up a thumb. He quickly disappeared into the back room again.

Aron wasn't sure what all that had been about. Belike Petror was giving the humans a chance to talk, he thought.

"Do you speak English?" He asked.

"Yes," she replied, with only the slightest accent to Aron's Anglish ears.

"My name's Aron."

"I'm Penny."

"Are you a friend of Petror? Or do you just work for him?"

Penny gave him a curious look that Aron couldn't figure out.

There was another awkward pause. This was cut short by Petror returning with another set of paperwork. Without sitting down, Aron signed the new documents.

"All done?" Aron asked.

"Yas. Farwell."

"Farewell. Maybe we'll see each other in the future."

"Yas! I hope I can sai you again," Petror said with a bright smile.

As Aron headed to the door, Penny did too. After he had stepped through the door, Aron held it open for her. She stepped out with only a glance back at Petror, who nodded at her meaningfully.

Aron wasn't quite sure if, culturally speaking, he owed her a farewell also. So he followed Petror's lead and nodded at her.

Then he headed back the way he had come. Penny also headed in that direction. She stopped right behind him when he stopped to check he hadn't forgotten anything. Aron was surprised. He continued on his way, and she followed.

About halfway across the square, he stopped and turned around.

"Are you following me?" He asked.

"Yes," she replied meekly.

"Why?" Aron asked, confused.

Now she looked confused. "I'm sorry?"

"Why are you following me?" He asked, not sure what the confusion was.

"I, uh...?" Penny stuttered. "Petror didn't tell you?"

"Tell me what?"

"He gave me to you as part of the trade."

"I'm sorry?"

"That last bit you signed was a slave transfer form – I'm yours now," Penny said. Then, just to be clear, she added, "I'm a slave."

Aron was shocked. Visibly so – he had never seen an enslaved person before in his life (that he knew of).

Penny was also somewhat shocked. "You didn't know? You signed it."

"I can't read Tungolese!" Aron exclaimed.

Aron's mind rushed through the emotions of disgust at the concept, fear of the consequences, and dreams of being a slave-freeing hero. But this eventually ended firmly back in fear.

"No, no. I can't have a slave," he said.

Aron headed back to the shop. Penny stayed outside. She'd just become free of Petror; she wouldn't go back unless she was expressly told to. It wasn't that Petror had been a bad master, but if her new owner was so against enslaving a person, there was a good chance he might free her. This was quite a happy thought. But she quickly reminded herself not to let her hopes run away with such a foolish fantasy.

Petror was somewhat surprised to see Aron back again.

"Is what you gave me a slave?" Aron asked.

"Yas," Petror said.

"I can't take a slave! They're illegal!"

"No dey not!" Petror said with a face full of disbelief.

"They are where I come from!"

"Vah! Wall, if you no want, you sall it. Dat is good too. It gat good price. 100 Drax, meybe 200 Drax."

"I don't think I should take it... her!"

Aron reached out to hand the device back to Petror.

"No, no, no!" Petror said. "It gift. You kaip it." He started quite literally pushing Aron to the door.

"It for you now," Petror said at the door. And with that, Aron was out on the street again.

He stood there momentarily as he considered whether he should try again.

"He won't change his mind," Penny said.

"Well, I can't take you with me. How about this? You're free to go. Can I do that?" Aron asked. He spoke at a volume that made Penny nervous.

"No. Not without releasing the slave-bolt," she said quietly, cautiously scanning their surroundings.

"What, this thing?" Aron asked, indicating the device that he held in his hand.

"It's a tiny metal device that looks like a bolt; here," Penny said, turning and pointing to a spot between her shoulder blades. "It's to keep slaves in line. That's the controller. But most people call that the slave-bolt."

"And the code that Petror showed me?"

"You have to enter that code every day. Otherwise, bad things happen," she said.

"Like what?" Aron asked, concerned.

"I don't know," Penny lied. Then she added, "I've never had it happen."

"Good thing I remember it, then. What if I just give you this?" Aron asked. He held the device out to her.

"I can't touch it." Penny shook her head and quickly withdrew her hands. "It'll shock me."

"Ok." Aron withdrew the device carefully. He stared at it for a moment. "Well, can I use this to free you?"

"I don't know," she replied. "I've never even heard of a freed slave."

Aron looked closer at the device.

"I can't read this. You can speak Tungolese, right? Can you read it?"

She shook her head. "I can speak Tun a little. I can't read it."

"Tun?"

"The main language of Tungol. It's called Tun. The second biggest language is Gol," Penny explained.

"Oh! Makes sense," Aron said. He looked at the device again as if it had some hidden answer. "We need to find someone to translate. I'll ask Petror."

"No! Not here!" She said forcefully but quietly, stopping Aron in his tracks.

"Why not?" He asked, surprised.

Penny quickly scanned their surroundings again. Then she spoke quietly. "They don't like freed slaves here. Once you're a slave, you're always a slave. People do bad things to wayward slaves. They're as likely to kill me as help you."

"Seriously?" Aron asked, almost in a whisper.

"Yes," she insisted.

"Man! Being a slave is maggoty! Belike it won't even have an option, then."

"It might. These aren't made here."

Aron stopped for a moment to think things through. "Well. I guess you're just going to have to come with me, then. We'll figure it out on the ship. Do you want to fetch your —" He stopped himself when he realised the potential foolishness of his question.

"The only thing I have is this dress, and I'm lucky Petror let me keep it. I like this dress," Penny replied as they started back towards the ship.

"What? He might have sent you off with nothing at all?" Aron asked, showing disdain.

"You can't have a slave naked on the streets. But slave owners normally hold on to the clothes when they sell a slave. I think Petror wanted to save you the effort of finding clothes for me. But he told me to put on the oldest thing I had."

Aron shook his head. "Why would they hold on to the clothes?"

"I don't know. That's just what happens. Petror gave me this when he bought us. Although it wasn't a dress, it was coveralls. It became a dress during some repairs."

"Who is 'us'?" Aron asked.

"Petror's other slave, Mathieu," Penny explained.

"That's right, he mentioned having two. Was that the other guy who came to the ship?"

"Yes," Penny said quickly.

"Does he not speak English? Or was I not supposed to talk to him or something?" Aron asked.

"You are allowed to talk to him. But he only speaks French and a little Tun."

Aron suddenly recalled something which Petror had said, stopping him in his tracks. Penny immediately and instinctively stopped beside him.

"Was he trying to ... breed you two?" Aron asked after trying and failing to come up with a way to tactfully ask that question.

"Yes," Penny said with a blush. "But Mathieu and I never actually tried. We just lied."

"All the same, that's —" Aron couldn't think of the appropriate adjective but failed. He shook his head and walked on.

—   —   —   —   —

When Aron and Penny were almost back at the ship, two Tungolese women appeared from around a distant corner and headed towards them.

Aron gave them a friendly wave while they were still some way off. "Hello."

"Gralu." One of them smiled in response.

"Musin," Penny said.

As they passed, one of the women deliberately bumped into Penny, her shoulder catching the bottom of Penny's rib cage. The two women giggled as they walked away. Aron noticed and thought about stopping the woman and saying something. But Penny shook her head at him. The women quickly disappeared around another corner, so Aron turned and walked on.

Marc was just completing the final tasks of loading the ship as Aron and Penny rounded the corner.

"Who were they?" Aron asked.

"I dunno. Just some overly friendly locals, I suppose. Couldn't understand a word of what they were saying," Marc said, not looking up from his work.

"So there were no issues with the other buyer?" Aron asked him.

"None," Marc said.

"And the new cargo is loaded and balanced?"

"Yep, all done, boss! It arrived while the second buyer was picking up his cargo. The sender wasn't particularly happy that we weren't ready to load his containers straight away."

"Well, that couldn't be helped," Aron sighed.

"I say we stick to transport-only shipments in the future," Marc suggested. "Buy-and-sell just carries too much risk."

"Agreed. What's that box off to the side?"

"This is my shopping! It was delivered here; I was worried it'd be late," Marc said. He immediately went to pick it up.

Aron was a bit concerned about what Marc may have bought. But given the situation, he decided not to press the issue.

"Well, let's get ready to go. We've been here too long already," Aron said.

Only after Marc put the box inside the door of the ship and turned around did he finally notice Penny standing there. "Oh! Who's this?"

"Uh..." Aron stuttered. "This is Penny. Penny, this is my brother, Marc. Penny will be coming with us."

"Coming with us?" Marc asked, confused.

"Yes. Is that a problem?" Aron asked in a vain attempt at avoiding the issue.

"No. But why?" Marc asked.

"Ah... She's sort of my slave," Aron admitted.

"What! What did you buy a slave for?" Marc yelled.

"I didn't buy a slave," Aron insisted. "I was given one by Petror."

"Petror?"

"The guy I was here with earlier. He thought this was a good way to compensate me for ruining the deal."

"Ok. But what are we going to do with her? You can't *actually* be thinking of taking her with us."

"You can't?" Penny asked, suddenly worried.

"The authorities back home don't take too kindly to people owning slaves," Marc said.

"Well, we can't leave her here either. We have to free her. We'll have to take her with us until we figure out how. Perhaps we'll be able to report it and get some form of amnesty," Aron suggested.

"I have heard of slaves being freed by the police before. But I don't think it works that way," Marc said.

"What do you mean?" Aron asked.

"I'm pretty sure they arrest people who 'accidentally' have slaves," Marc explained. "I mean, what would you say if you were caught with one?"

"Well, maybe we could call them in advance?"

"From where? You can't call from outside our home space. And they'll probably ask when we get stopped at the border."

"Maybe we'll be lucky and get through without being stopped," Aron said.

Aron and Marc headed towards the ship. Aron motioned for Penny to follow them.

"Maybe, but I wouldn't count on your luck," Marc said.

"Maybe I should stay here," Penny said, standing firm. "You could sell me to someone."

Aron and Marc stopped and looked at each other.

"We couldn't do that," Aron said, still looking at Marc for some confirmation.

"No," Marc agreed.

"You're coming with us," Aron said, talking to Penny. "We just have to figure out what to do."

—   —   —   —   —

"Welcome aboard the Eastern Light. This is your new home, for the moment," Aron said as they boarded. "This is the galley; basic cooking —"

"**Very** basic," Marc corrected as he dropped into a chair and started poking at a tablet computer.

"— and eating facilities and computer terminals for entertainment, work, communication, or whatever. That door is the shower, and that one is the dunny."

"The what?" Penny asked.

"The toilet," Marc explained.

"Through that door are the beds. The cargo hold is through the other door in the bedroom. The bedroom door isn't soundproof, so don't talk too loud. Fortunately, there are four beds, so we have a spare one for you. Although, we'll have to move Hana's crap."

"Is that the third person?" Penny asked.

"Yeah. Her name's, well, Hana. She's a friend of ours and the third pilot and best cook. But don't ask her to cook for you."

"She'll get upset?"

"No, it's much worse than that. She'll be happy to," Marc said. Aron nodded.

"Is that a problem?"

"Not if you've got a larger pair of pants handy," Marc laughed.

"Not a problem you're likely to have any time soon, in any case. We only have the rehydratable food at the moment," Aron said.

"A moment that's lasted months, Aron," Marc pointed out.

"I am aware," Aron sighed.

"So you're all pilots?" Penny asked.

"Technically, we're all pilots, cooks, mechanics, whatever. Small crew, so you do what you need to," Aron said.

"At least, whatever Captain Aron tells you to do," Marc added. "Not that it's as bad as being a slave!" He quickly added.

Penny laughed a little.

"Anyway, the only other thing is up there: the cockpit."

"It's a bit depressing when you can give a complete tour of your living quarters without taking a single step," Marc commented.

"It is cramped," Aron said. "But it's serviceable."

"It's nice," Penny said.

"Well, no. It's a bit maggoty. But it's our ... Uh oh," Marc said.

"What?"

"You know how I said the police have freed slaves? Not very successfully, as it turns out."

Marc turned the tablet so the others could see. It was a video of a formerly enslaved person who was now confined to a wheelchair: an unfortunate side-effect of the forced removal of the slave-bolt implant.

"This is their best attempt so far," Marc said, cringing.

Penny was shocked.

"It's alright, I think," Aron said. "I mean, I think this controller thing will have an option to free her."

"Really? Why don't you—" Marc started.

Aron anticipated the question. "I would, but it's all in gobbledegook," he said.

"Ah."

"We'll just have to find someone to help us," Aron said.

"Why don't you ask around here?" Marc asked.

"Not the done thing, apparently. As soon as you're ready —" Aron hinted, "— you can take us out."

"Beadful?" Marc asked. He stood up, ready to head for the cockpit.

"Beadful," Aron replied.

"This is exciting," Penny said.

"You've never been off Tungol?" Aron asked, surprised.

"I wasn't born there. But I thought I'd never leave."

"Well then! Take the co-pilot's seat. You can watch it disappear from view. Hopefully, the last time in your life!"

Penny excitedly ran forward and took the seat to Marc's left. Aron stood behind to help monitor the instruments.

Penny watched as the spaceport shrank away from the ship before fading into invisibility. Once everything outside was dark, with Marc's guidance, she switched to watching the console and watched the navigation icon for Tungol slide quickly off the bottom of the navigation screen.

"It's gone!" She breathed.

"Yep," Aron said. "You're free!"

I can't sleep.
Don't worry, honey. Jess and I will protect you from the monsters.
There are Monsters!
Good evening! Evie?

29 sleepers, 7 goners, Cap. A couple of nice 'apprentices'!
Batches of 10, Reth.
Evie, I'd like a word.
Name?
Joyce.
No, your name is Dime.
Name?
Jason.
No, yours is Grand.
Why do you ask? You don't care!
'Cause I'm a scunner. You're Bob.
I want my ring back!
Ha!
I'm going to call you Dough, pork-chop.
Maggot-brain!
You're Bill.
I'm Michael.
You're Bill or I beat you.
And the little one will be Penny.

Episode II. Pirate Problems

"I miss out on all the excitement," Hana complained dejectedly, having just walked up to the cockpit from the bedroom.

"Were you watching her sleep? That's weird!" Aron said, turning briefly from the controls.

"I was not ... I was just curious," Hana said with a guilty look.

"She's a good sleeper. She went to bed the same time I did."

"I don't think she slept, though. I'm pretty sure she was awake when I woke up."

"I did think it would be a little early for her. It would have been late afternoon on the Tungol spaceport."

"Yeah. Plus, it's a bit of a change of circumstances for her. She must have had a lot to think about," Hana said. Then, out of nowhere, she added, "This is the first time I've met a slave."

"I think that's true for all of us," Aron chuckled.

"Do you think they are common on Tungol?" Hana asked quickly.

"I think it's something like every second person is a slave."

"That's a lot!" Hana said a bit too loudly. She turned quickly to make sure she hadn't woken anybody up.

"At least, that's what I read somewhere. I don't know how accurate it is. You can't trust everything you read."

"How much is a slave worth?" She asked.

"I think Petror said 200 Drax, which is —"

"What! That's nearly ten thousand credits!"

"Yeah, I'm not sure if he meant 200 or two-zero-zero in base 12. That would be something like 260, 300 Drax."

Hana stopped and did the math. "288. Whatever the base, we could do a lot with that much money!"

"We're not selling her!" Aron said firmly, cutting off any ideas Hana might have formed.

"Of course not!" Hana responded indignantly.

"Just making sure that's clear. Petror might think he gifted her to me, but I don't believe people can own people. So really, she's not a slave anymore," he said with conviction.

"She's still tied to this thing. That makes her a slave no matter what you think about it," Hana said, picking up the slave-bolt controller.

"Yeah, well, if the police find us with that, you might still get your excitement," Aron said, then added, "Don't play with it. It can do bad things, from what I am told."

"I'm not going to shock her or anything," Hana said defensively.

"You can't read it. How would you even know what you were doing?"

"I'm not even touching anything," she said. To emphasise the point, she made a show of putting it down gently. "Why are you so uptight all of a sudden? This is not like you."

"Sorry. I guess I am. There's a high alert for pirates in this sector," Aron sighed.

"So what?" Hana asked.

"And we've got a ship following us."

Aron pointed to a blip on his instruments.

"That one? It's been there for a while. You can't say it's following us when we're on a major route."

"It's hardly a major route. In any case, why is it sticking so close? There's plenty of spaceway."

"Relax! You're just being paranoid. You'll see, when we get to the waypoint, they won't follow us down the Beadful corridor."

Aron wasn't so easily convinced. "I'm not so sure."

"We're not going to run into pirates! I mean, have you ever even —"

"Have I ever?" Aron asked incredulously.

He spoke a little too loud, and they heard a slight groan from one of the two occupied beds. They went silent for a moment, hoping they hadn't woken someone up. Hana crept back and slid the bedroom door closed.

"That was one time. And it was years ago!" Hana whispered.

"Yeah," Aron sighed.

"You've never told me what really happened, anyway," Hana said.

"First job out of high school. I was working on a large passenger ship during the summer break. It was just one flight to earn a bit of spending money. And I chose that flight because it was on the way back from my family's usual vacation spot. Anyway, apparently one of the passengers was a mole. One night when we were out in deep space, she killed the watch officer and tried to dock a small ship, presumably with more people. Fortunately, the cook noticed and managed to subdue her. The small ship was long gone before the authorities arrived, though."

"Did you know it was happening?" Hana asked, quietly absorbing what he'd said.

"Not until after."

"How come you haven't told me about this before? I told you about the time I was robbed."

"You had someone pinch a bag with your lunch in it while you were in another room. It's not the same. I don't know. It was kind of traumatic."

"Isn't that a bit over the top? You didn't even know! I mean, mayhaps they were just going to board and then steal all the valuable stuff."

"They don't go to such effort just to steal a few trinkets," Aron said matter-of-factly.

"How would you know what they would do? You and your brother are goody-goody church boys."

"You go to church."

"Yeah, but I'm not a goody-goody. You guys wouldn't know the first thing about the thinking of a criminal."

"He's right," came a small voice from behind them.

It made Hana jump. "Penny! You gave me a fright!" She said.

"Sorry!" Penny said quite emphatically. She slid the bedroom door closed behind her and walked to the front of the ship.

"Don't worry about it! I'm just not used to having an extra person on board. Hi! I'm Hana."

"I'm, uh, Penny," Penny replied, surprised by the unnecessary introductions.

"Oh, I know. I realised a little too late that it was silly to introduce ourselves. But still, welcome to the ship! It's great having another woman on board."

"Calm down, Hana. Don't smother her," Aron said.

"Sorry," Hana said. But then she immediately switched back into high gear. "Do you want anything? We have all the flavours of rehydratable food."

"Except egg," Aron clarified.

"Yes, except egg. Aron doesn't like egg flavour."

"Me? What about you?" He asked.

"I can eat it."

"That's not what you told me."

"Well, I don't love it. Depends on my mood. It reminds me of the stinker," Hana said. "The 'Stinker' was an old ship I used to work on. Smelled of —"

Aron interrupted Hana before she completed that sentence. "I thought you were getting her something to eat."

"I am!" Hana said, surprised by the interruption.

"Well then, belike it's not a good idea to fill her head with thoughts of bad smells," Aron said.

"Oh, right. Penny, come. Let's get you something to eat."

Hana jumped from her seat and led Penny to the small kitchenette.

"Did you want anything, Aron?" Hana asked.

"Can you get me a coffee?" Aron yelled back to her.

"Sure, no problem."

She turned and took another look at Penny as she started pulling packets of food out of a cupboard.

"And we'll have to get you something better to wear," she said. "I mean, it's pretty clear your old owner didn't have the slightest idea about what's feminal. And those are definitely not fain!"

"Hey! Those clothes are mine," Aron called back.

"Oh. I thought they looked familiar! Why did you give her your clothes?"

"Well, what she was wearing was falling apart. And I didn't want to give her your stuff without your permission."

"I hope you gave her clean stuff," Hana said.

"What do you mean? I clean my stuff more often than you do!"

Hana had momentarily forgotten that she had been getting food by this point. She had headed back towards her locker to look for clothes.

"Don't worry, Penny. I'll take you shopping when we land next, and I'll buy you some nice new stuff of your own. But you can borrow some of mine for now."

"I don't need anything fancy," Penny said.

"I'm not talking about anything fancy. I don't particularly like fancy clothes either. Besides, there's no point in having fancy clothes on a freight ship. They're not comfortable enough for work. And the only people who'll see what you wear will have also seen you wearing your pyjamas. But we should get you something for special occasions."

"You'll have to give up one of your lockers if you're buying her stuff. You can't have two now that there are four of us."

"Right. It's fain. I'll find a way to squeeze them in one," Hana said, opening one of the lockers and pulling things out. She laid a few choices of shirts and pants out on the bench. "Which do you like?"

"They all look good," Penny said.

"Ok, well, just pick something."

Penny looked unsure, so Hana eventually made a choice for her. She then ushered Penny into the shower to change. When Penny emerged, Hana sent her back in again with another top because she'd changed her mind while putting the other clothes away.

"Oh, is this Penny's dress?" Hana asked, finding it hanging over the end of Penny's bed.

"Whose else would it be?" Aron asked.

"This is so tatty," she said as Penny emerged again. "I guess we can throw this out now."

"No. Please don't. It's the only thing I have. I've had it for years."

"But it's stained and ripped in all sorts of places. Look, it's been stitched back together from the hem to the armpit!"

"Hana!" Aron snapped.

"Fine!" Hana sighed.

"They used to be coveralls," Penny mentioned quietly.

"What?" Hana laughed. "How? It goes down to your knees as a dress, and I can't see any stitching down the middle."

"The Tungol slave merchants sell these coveralls with long middle sections and short, baggy legs. That way, it fits almost everybody; you just bunch up the excess in the middle and tie the belt around it. It tore across the back, so I needed a large bit of fabric to fix it up. So I used one of the legs. But it looked silly with one leg, so I turned it into a dress."

"How long was it originally?"

"On a human, they're pretty much the right size. A tall human might have their ankles exposed, though. The legs didn't even come up as far as my knees, so cutting them off left me with a decent length for a dress."

"Ok, I see what you mean," Hana said, inspecting the dress again.

It was at this point that she remembered she had been preparing food. She almost dropped the dress as she hurried Penny back to the kitchen. Then she reopened the small cupboard door in the kitchen and extracted a few more of the silver packets. She shuffled through them quickly, pulling out specific ones and putting them on the bench. Then she dumped the others back into the cupboard without any particular care.

"What would you like?" Hana asked, waving her hand over the selections she'd made.

"What are the options?" Penny asked, staring at the food.

"I'm sorry. You probably don't know how to read. Do you?"

"I do. But I don't know what 'ge-no-chi' is."

"Ah. That's gnocchi. It's a sort of potato-pasta thing. That rehydrates pretty well."

Hana pointed to and named each of the other options in turn and let Penny choose one. Penny wasn't sure what to choose, so she took the gnocchi.

"Just wait a moment, and I'll do that for you," Hana said as she turned her attention to Aron's coffee.

"I'm sure she's capable of doing it herself. She doesn't need you to do it for her," Aron interjected.

"Ok, fine," Hana said defensively.

"What do I do with this?" Penny asked Hana quietly.

"Dump it in a bowl (in that drawer), and then chuck it in the conveam," Hana whispered back.

Penny opened the drawer and found a blue bowl. Then she tore open the silver packet and dumped its contents into the bowl. The pasta had a powdery surface and did not look at all appealing. But she placed the bowl into the glass-fronted cooking appliance that Hana had pointed at.

"How does it work?" Penny asked.

Hana thought about this for a moment, which Penny thought odd. "I don't remember the explanation," she finally responded. "It just heats and hydrates the food; that's all I know."

Penny gave a small laugh. "No, I mean, how do I work **this model**?"

"Oh! You can just set it to auto. Here, watch me," Hana said, demonstrating the controls.

"Thanks," Penny said.

Once it was cooked, the conveam beeped. Penny removed her food and found it looked surprisingly edible now that it had been heated and hydrated.

Meanwhile, Hana had turned to Aron as she started making his coffee. "You'll have to give me the money for the new clothes, though. I don't have any."

"If I'm giving you the money, aren't I really buying the clothes?" Aron asked over his shoulder.

"You should be buying the clothes! I mean, she is technically your slave."

"Don't say that!" Aron cried.

"What? It is technically your responsibility."

"No. It's not that I mind paying for the clothes. Just don't call Penny a slave. She's not a slave."

"I'm just saying. Sorry, Penny."

"I don't mind, really!" Penny said. "It's just a word. I've been called worse things."

"Well, I mind!" Aron said.

"Why?" Hana asked.

"I don't know. I just do. A person is not a slave; they are just a person. A person that other people have mistreated. And if you call her a slave, you're making me be one of those people."

"I should buy the clothes," Penny declared. "I mean, obviously, I don't have money. But if they're for me, and if I'm free now, then I should be the one to pay Aron back."

"If you want to pay for the clothes, we can work out a way to do that," Aron said.

"No, don't make her pay! I mean, be practical; how is she even supposed to do that?" Hana said.

"I could work for the money. I'm sure there are jobs on this ship I could do. I want to earn my own way. I really don't want to be a burden to all of you."

"Penny, you're not a burden to us," Aron said. "But if you want to help out, that's great. We can always use the help."

"But also, Penny, you can expect some help every now and then," Hana said. "Now, what was I doing again?"

"You were making me coffee," Aron said.

"What! Maybe you should make it yourself! I'm not your slave!" Hana snorted.

"What?" Aron started.

"I'm sure you are capable of doing it yourself. You don't need me to do it for you."

"Hana, I'm flying," Aron said.

"I know. I'm just joking around. I'm already doing it," Hana laughed. "Making myself one, too."

With the coffee done, Hana balanced her plate of food on her arm and took a coffee cup in each hand. Then she headed to the cockpit. Penny followed a step behind.

Aron took a sip from his coffee and was struck by a thought.

"Penny, what were you saying before?" He asked Penny.

"When?" Hana asked.

"Not you; I'm talking to Penny."

"About working?" Penny asked, confused.

"No, sorry, I realise we've said a lot since then. I meant when we were talking about pirates before, you started to say something."

It took Penny a moment to think back.

"Oh. It's just that you were right. If pirates are just trying to rob the ship, they don't tend to use inside men. Because they don't care so much if they cut through the hull and kill the people inside. And thieves aren't likely to hit a passenger ship. They prefer merchantmen to passenger ships. It was more likely they were slavers," she explained.

"What? What makes you say that?" Hana asked, surprised by the innocent-looking girl's knowledge of the darker elements of the universe.

"Well, I was too young to be sold on the market when I was captured, so I spent the first 14 years with the slavers."

Aron was speechless. Hana was not.

"That must have been maggoty! What was it like?" She asked.

"Pretty difficult. But Bill, one of the other slaves, took care of me. And one of the slavers, Jor, as well. He was the main adult looking after us kids."

"Did they treat you badly?" Aron asked.

"Ignored, mostly, so long as I did my work. Slavers don't have time for a little girl, except if they're drunk and lonely. But I was ok because there were people around to protect me. Particularly the Captain; he didn't care about us, but he protected his 'investments'."

"How did you get there? I mean, were you kidnapped? Were your parents captured, too?" Hana asked.

Hana seemed oblivious to the grave expression on Penny's face. Aron gave her a nudge.

"Hana, maybe she doesn't want to talk about it anymore," he suggested.

"No, it's ok. I can talk about it, I think," Penny said. She took a breath before she spoke. "I don't really remember my parents except, uh, images. I was five when I was taken. I was travelling with friends of my parents. The ship was taken at night: they'd put the 'hook' (that's what they call the inside man) on before we departed. And then, one night, she pumped a sleeping gas through the vents. And the next thing we knew, we were waking up in a holding cell. They gave us all new names, implanted us with the slave bolts, sold off all the adults, and then it was just me and Bill left on the ship with them."

"That must have been a terrible ordeal!" Hana gasped.

"I don't really remember much of it. Just a few things. Like waking up to the loud voices and Bill looking after me. The rest is just what I was told by Bill. And it could have been worse. Usually, a few people die getting the slave bolt put in. Or are paralysed (but might as well have died). But that didn't happen to me or anyone from my ship."

Hana and Aron shared a shocked look.

"And Jor took care to look after us," Penny added.

"What was he like? Or is Jor a woman?" Aron asked.

"Ha! He was a big muscley man, always playing with his glasses. And he was good with Bill and me. Normally pirates don't keep kids as they can't sell them. But then the Captain kept Bill and me, calling us' investments'. But he never showed much interest in us. Jor was the one that did most of the actual work looking after us. Of course, we did most of the cooking and cleaning."

"Did you ever go on any pirate raids?" Hana asked with sudden energy.

"No. I never left the base. That was all done by a couple of pirates led by the Captain. Oh, and Ciny, who would go on board to gas the ... victims. I'm surprised the woman on your ship didn't use gas."

"Maybe it was too expensive?" Hana suggested.

"It's not, actually," Penny stated.

"She might have tried," Aron said, thinking about it. "I think they said she hit someone with a gas bottle. I had just assumed it had been nearby."

"Ok, but—" Hana started, but Aron interrupted her.

"Hana, I think we should give Penny a break. She's barely had a chance to eat! Why don't you tell her a bit about yourself?"

"Uh." Hana sputtered, suddenly feeling self-conscious. "I don't know; you go first."

"What? Fine. I grew up with my parents and Marc on Angish in Morton Creek. Uh, I went to university with Hana. Bob was there, too. I worked on various ships for a while, then saved up and bought this ship about a year ago. Hana and my brother tagged along," Aron said quickly. "Now, your turn."

"Well, Aron spoilt the ending to mine, but I grew up on Angish Spaceport—" Hana started.

But Aron shushed her.

"What?" She asked.

"Did you hear something?"

"Like what?" Hana asked, surprised.

"Something was banging aft on the hull," Aron stated, pointing towards the ship's rear.

"Belike something fell down in the hold," Hana said calmly.

"We're hours out of port. Anything that might have fallen would surely have done so by now. It's not like something could vibrate loose."

Hana slapped the back of his shoulder. "You're being paranoid again."

Aron was about to respond when they heard two distinct (yet not loud) clangs from the rear of the ship.

"Paranoid, am I?"

"What was that?" Hana asked, suddenly serious.

"I don't know," Aron said quietly. "Mayhaps it was someone landing on the outside of the ship?"

"What do we do?"

"I'm going to have a look," he said, suddenly standing up.

"You're going outside?" She asked, pushing him back down.

"No, I'm going to the hold," he explained.

"Should I come too?"

"You stay here and watch the controls. Penny can stay here too."

"Wake Marc and take him with you."

Aron thought about this.

"I'll have a quick look first."

He stood up out of the pilot's chair and signalled for Hana to take his spot.

"What if there's someone there?" Hana asked as she sat down and cast her eye over the instruments.

"They can't have come through the airlock. The alarms would have gone off. I'm just going to look."

Aron crept slowly to the back door of the cabin. He briefly paused as he passed the bunks, reconsidering whether to wake Marc. Deciding against it, he opened the door to the hold and went through.

The hold was silent, which Aron thought to be a good thing. The only sounds were those made by Aron as he moved around. But it currently held over two thousand minicrates which obstructed his view of the outside walls. They were stacked in two blocks, with walking space on either side and a wide aisle for the loading robots down the middle. The central space was obviously clear. Aron was suddenly nervous about being in this big room all by himself. Aron reasoned that if someone had breached the ship, they could get behind him by sneaking down one side while he was on the other. On the other hand, perhaps

Aron could be the one to be the sneak. He could head down one side of the hold and check if the airlock had been breached.

"Aron, you're being ridiculous," he whispered to himself.

He moved to the port side of the ship and looked down the side aisle. Seeing nothing there, he headed to the other side and checked. When he saw that that aisle was also empty, he crept down it to the back of the ship. Once there, he tiptoed towards the airlock door. Then he paused, caught his breath, and stopped to listen for a few moments. Hearing nothing, he opened the door and cautiously looked inside. It was empty. He left the door open. The safety mechanisms would prevent the outer door from being opened if the inner door wasn't closed. Aron hoped that would prevent anyone from forcing their way through the airlock.

Then he quickly, but still quietly, made his way back to the front of the hold via the central aisle. Aron locked the door to the hold after passing through it. Then he headed back to where Hana and Penny were nervously waiting.

"What did you see?" Hana asked.

"Nothing. I couldn't hear anything, either," he replied, standing behind Hana's chair. "I left the inner door to the airlock open so that nobody can come in that way."

"What if they force the outer door?" Hana asked.

"If they force the door, belike the expulsion of all the air from the hold will blow them away."

"And if it doesn't."

"Well, the air pressure would make the cabin's back door almost impossible to open," Aron explained. "I locked that door anyway, just in case they do manage to get in somehow."

"In that situation, they'd already managed to open or bypass the airlock door. They could do something similar to the cabin door."

"Only hypothetically."

Hana couldn't think of any other objections. She just gave Aron a concerned look.

"They might not care about blowing the airlocks and doors," Penny said quietly, breathing a little faster and heavier. "They could just be after the goods."

"Well, it wouldn't be the worst thing. The insurance would cover that, right?" Hana asked.

"Belike it would," Aron said.

"The insurance doesn't matter if we're dead!" Penny said abruptly.

Aron and Hana were shocked into silence by Penny's sudden outbreak.

"I told you, thieves don't care about venting the air and killing people," she explained. "People cause problems for thieves. Slavers won't kill us, but they would be trying to pump gas into the life support. If thieves can't open a door, they just cut a hole in it and damn whoever is inside breathing the air."

"What do we do?" Hana asked. Nobody answered, so she added with a bit more urgency, "Anyone?"

Aron thought about this. "We can use the R.D. to have a look. Then we at least know what's going on outside. I'll do that. Hana, you keep flying. Penny, uh, wake Marc. He can keep an eye on the airlock."

Aron was already moving. He set himself down in the co-pilot's chair and started frantically punching the controls.

Penny was a little unsure about waking Marc. But she sheepishly opened the door to his bunk and poked him in the shoulder.

"What's going on?" He asked in a daze.

"We think someone's on the outside of the ship," Penny said quietly.

Marc quickly got out of his bunk and walked up to the cockpit.

"Someone's on the ship?"

"We think so."

"What makes you say that?"

"Two things. First, we may be being followed," Aron said.

"Or not. We're not sure on that one," Hana said.

"That ship?" Marc asked, pointing at a screen.

"Yeah."

"That's a short-range ship crewed by a couple of Tungolese women. I saw it at the spaceport; they docked next door. Pretty sure its cargo is little fluffy bunnies or something," Marc stated.

"We also heard noises on the hull. Banging noises," Hana said.

Marc seemed disconcerted by that. "That... that could be something."

"I'm checking it out with the R.D. Can you keep an eye on the airlock? Let us know if it sounds like someone is outside or trying to get in," Aron said.

"Sure," Marc agreed. He headed to the back of the ship.

"What's an R.D.?" Penny asked after he had gone.

"Remote Repair and Diagnostic Device. It's a camera and an arm that you can move to make simple repairs outside the ship," Aron said, still focused on the display.

"Have you seen anything?" Hana asked.

"Nothing. But this thing is pretty slow."

Aron kept moving the robot around. Hana kept glancing over at Aron's screen more often than she should have. Penny had nothing to do and just sat there nervously, waiting for some news.

"Look—" Aron started. But he was interrupted by Marc reentering the cabin.

"What is it?" Aron asked him.

"I haven't heard anything back there; just the R.D. as it moves around. Have you seen anything?"

"I was just about to say: something knocked the new radio antenna off its mount," Aron said.

"That doesn't mean there's someone on the ship," Marc said. "More likely, it was a bit of debris. Belike that was the source of the noise, though."

"Belike. I haven't checked the port side yet."

"What about underneath?" Hana asked.

"There's not going to be anything," Marc sighed. "You guys are overreacting to nothing."

"Let's wait until we've had a look," Hana said.

"Fine. You do that. I'm going back to bed," Marc said. He headed back to his bunk and practically dropped into the bed.

"This is why I didn't want to wake him up," Aron whispered.

"Because he'd talk some sense into us?" Hana whispered back.

"It's not that he does it; it's the way he does it."

"Yeah, well, he's your brother," she sighed.

"Doesn't that make it worse?"

"Yep," she laughed.

"There's definitely nobody on the outside of the ship," Aron said with a sigh.

"Well, that's good news. Do you want to take over the controls again? I'll park the R.D.," Hana said.

"Sure."

With a display of well-rehearsed awkwardness, Hana and Aron swapped seats.

"Sorry," Penny said.

"For what?" Aron asked.

"For freaking you out."

"Relax!" Hana said. "We are perfectly capable of doing that to ourselves. At worst, you just hurried it along."

"And don't apologise for being scared," Aron added. "No matter what Marc says. Sometimes it's prudent."

There were a few moments of silence as Aron and Hana concentrated on their tasks.

"How are you doing, Penny?" Hana asked over her shoulder.

"Fine."

"Do you know how to play Hehed Party?"

"I don't know how to play anything," Penny laughed nervously.

"Well, that's good. I'm going to teach you," Hana smiled.

"Maybe she needs a better teacher," Aron said with a smirk.

"Maybe you should be quiet!" Hana said, standing up and giving Aron a playful punch on the shoulder.

"Yeah. Quiet is good," Aron said to himself.

Time for the implants. You're first, Chip!
Your turn, Quid.
This one is handsome!

Come now, Bob.
How is Jason?
It's Grand.
He's alive.
Now go.
My turn now?
You're too small, little ones.
Come, eat.
Your friends have survived.

Episode III. Passkey Panic

"I'm hungry," Hana whined.

"So eat," Aron said.

"Ugh. But there's only dehydrated bacon and egg," she said, flopping her hands dramatically. "When are we stopping next?"

"You know the schedule. It won't be in the next few hours, so you're just going to deal with bacon and egg."

"Can we do something fun when we get there?" She asked.

"You can do something if you want. The second delivery is going to be late, so we'll be there for four days now. But I'm going to stay put and save my money."

"Four days! I don't think we've ever stayed that long in a port. You know, holidays aside."

"Yeah, well, I don't like it," Aron sighed. "Things don't stop costing money just because we've stopped moving."

"We can do something that doesn't cost us anything. There are bushwalking trails and stuff, from what I read. Penny would like that, I think."

"She might hate it," Aron laughed.

"You mean you'd hate it," she said, poking him.

"No, I like bushwalking."

"Have you ever been bushwalking?"

"I went with Hahaha up Mount Polinski," Aron said.

"What! Why didn't you take me?" Hana asked, scandalised.

"You were working on that stinker at the time."

"Ah! The stinker—" She shuddered at the memory. "You know, the stinker always had good food."

"You hated the stinker!"

"Yeah. I couldn't take the smell. But the food was good," she thought again about the food, then shuddered when she remembered the smell. "No, this will always be better than the stinker."

"Anyway, you promised to take Penny shopping."

"We can *easily* do both. We've got *four days*!" Hana gushed. "I'm going to look up walks that we can do."

She jumped out of her seat excitedly.

"I thought you were hungry," Aron laughed.

"I can eat while I read. It'll take my mind off the egg and bacon flavour," she laughed.

— — — — —

Their first day on Beadful was short and busy. They docked at the Ophir Spaceport very late in the local afternoon. They spent what remained of the daylight unloading their cargo. However, nightfall at Ophir was near the middle of the day for Aron and something akin to mid-morning for Penny. But Hana needed to sleep, so Marc and Aron decided to take Penny on a quick walk out on the spaceport to let Hana have some quiet.

"How are you adjusting to life on the ship?" Marc asked Penny.

"I'm not sure that I am," Penny responded. "I can't seem to settle on a sleep schedule."

"Yeah, that's difficult," Aron said. Marc nodded.

"I thought it would be easier to try to match Aron's schedule, given it is close to what I was used to on Tungol. But I can't get myself to sleep that early. So then I try to stay awake later to make myself tired, and that doesn't work either."

"You just have to pick a schedule and stick to it. You'll adapt eventually," Marc said.

"Belike. Hana is insistent that I switch to her schedule. But that'd be a huge change!" Penny said.

"Just ignore her, do what is best for you," Marc said. "Have you done much travelling, Penny?"

"I was travelling somewhere when the slavers got me," Penny said. "I don't know where, though. But since then, the only places I've seen were the slavers' base, their delivery ship, Tungol slave market, and wherever on Tungol Spaceport Petror had errands."

"Well, now you can add our ship and Beadful Spaceport," Marc said.

"Ophir Spaceport. Beadful Spaceport is on the other side of the planet."

"It's *a* Beadful spaceport. In fact, it's the largest one," Marc said.

"It's not *the* Beadful Spaceport," Aron countered. "But, you're right, Beadful Spaceport is nothing special. Just basic docks, from what I hear."

"Where are we headed, anyway?" Marc asked, cutting Aron's explanation short.

"I was planning on just going to the end of the row and back. Apparently, there is a windowed area at the end with a view of the planet."

"That sounds good," Penny said.

"It might be. But they're often filled with rubbish and broken things that freighters just dump," Marc said.

"Sounds like the Tungol Spaceport," Penny stated.

"That's pretty much every spaceport," said Marc. "They get so many transient visitors that don't care; they just dump and go."

Sure enough, the open space at the end of the row was almost entirely full of discarded crates. (Given the faded state of the printing on them, they'd been there for some time.) At some point in the past, someone had cleared a path through the boxes to the window. It was a tight squeeze on the way in, and once the three of them were at the window there was barely any elbow room. But the view was worth any inconvenience. The sun had just dipped below the horizon. Though the planet below them was dark, the atmosphere glowed in a thin arc at the horizon in bright blue, white, and orange layers. A keen eye could just make out the shape of the mountains along the horizon.

"Well, that's boring. I'd hoped we be in time to catch the end of the sunset," Marc said.

"I think it's beautiful!" Penny said.

"Sure, it has some beauty. But it must be pretty much the same as a night on Tungol."

"I never saw that. I'm not sure I ever had a good look at the planet. I certainly never left Petror's shop after sunset."

"Oh," Marc went quiet to let Penny enjoy the scene. It also gave him time to digest this information.

After a few minutes, they decided to move on. But all they found from that point were more docks, so they headed back to the ship.

— — — — —

As soon as Hana was awake, she started talking about going on the bush walk she had planned. But at this point, Aron was about to sleep for his scheduled night. He suggested that they hold off until the next day so that he could shift his sleep cycle slightly to be able to go on the walk with her. In place of the walk, Hana decided she would take Penny to the spaceport's shopping precinct in search of clothing. Hana convinced Aron to come, promising it would be a short trip. She also promised it would be an excellent way to shift his sleep cycle by preventing him from sleeping too early.

"I need to sit down!" Aron groaned after only a little more than an hour. "I should be asleep by now."

"Yeah, sorry, but we can't go back yet. But we can take a break," Hana said.

"Haven't we bought enow already?" Aron asked.

"We have all the basic, everyday stuff," Hana said. "But I want to get something a bit more sensible."

"Like business wear?" Penny asked.

"Not only for business. But something like that," Hana said.

Hana took them on a bee-line for the food court.

"So, what is this place?" Penny asked Hana as they saved a table while Aron was queuing to order coffee.

"Ophir Spaceport, on Beadful. Beadful is a bit weird because it was originally a colony from Earth but isn't a part of the Tuanti. So lots of things are different. Like the laws are different. And you have to go through customs."

"What's the Tuanti?"

"It's just the top-level government of all the – well, most of the planets with human settlement. Planets don't have to be part of it, though. Like they have to vote to be part of it or leave it. I think that makes it a confederation. Or is that just a federation?"

Penny shrugged, not sure why it was even important.

Hana threw her hands in the air. "I don't know; I was never good at history or politics. Aron, you tell her."

"About?" Aron asked, having only just arrived and missed the preceding discussion.

"About the Tuanti."

"Well, for a start, it's not history; it's current," Aron said, dropping into a chair with a table marker.

"Whatever," Hana said dismissively.

"Anyway, was there a specific question?"

"She asked about Beadful and the Tuanti," Hana said.

"Oh, Beadful's a bit weird. It's the only Earth colony that is not part of the Tuanti."

"Exactly what I said," Hana laughed.

"Oh, ok. Uh, what else do you want to know, Penny?"

"Anything you can tell me."

"Alright. It was settled by Xian monks, who still control most of the planet. Most of it has been left as natural forests. Where it is populated, the people are pretty religious. But Ophir is different as it was founded separately on land leased from the Xian government for 99 years. So Ophir has its own government and has some pretty lax laws. Which is good for us at the moment."

"Slavery is still illegal, though. Isn't it?" Hana asked.

"It's still illegal. But nobody's going to be actively looking here, I think."

"Is the Tuanti bad?" Penny asked.

"Why would it be bad?" Hana asked.

"The slavers never had anything good to say about it," Penny responded.

"That isn't surprising. The authorities are not inclined to be lenient towards law-breakers," Aron said. "But that's something for us to be scared of in the not too distant future."

"What *are* we going to do? We're supposed to be heading that way in a few days," Hana asked.

"We're headed to Dwanty next," Aron corrected her.

"Oh. They sound so similar. I thought you said 'Tuanti'."

"Why would I say that? I'd tell you the planet if we were going there!"

"I wasn't really listening. But anyway, that only delays the problem."

"Well, I have two possible plans for getting past the checkpoints," Aron said with fake enthusiasm.

"Go on," Hana said sceptically.

"One, we go for one of the busier checkpoints and hope we don't get picked," Aron said.

"You'd need to be very lucky for that," Hana said, rolling her eyes.

"Right. The other possibility is to go for one of the small checkpoints and hope it's closed."

"Yeah, that's not much better."

"Don't just criticise. What's your plan?" Aron asked, leaning back into his chair.

"I don't have one," she said outright.

"Yeah, there are no easy answers," He sighed.

"Can we get around the checkpoints somehow?" Hana asked.

"I really don't think so. If you could go through without any checks, everyone would do it. Even when you're legal, they're a pain," Aron said.

"Can we go to a smaller checkpoint, and if it's open, turn around?"

Aron shook his head. "By the time we know if it's open, it's too late. If we turn around, they'll flag it as suspicious, and we'd always be stopped for checks in the future."

"Hmm... Penny, do you know a way? Any tricks you learned while living with the pirates?" Hana asked.

"I think they had ways. They didn't really tell me any of their secrets, though," Penny said. "I only saw what happened when they got back from their runs."

Now it was Hana's turn to slump back into her chair.

"If we can't get through with a slave, maybe we can free Penny first. Do you think we could find a translator for the device?" Hana asked.

"No good," Aron said. "They pay bounties for reporting crimes here. You could never trust someone with that information."

"I thought you said the laws were lax?" Hana said, surprised.

Aron hushed her for a moment as his coffee was delivered to the table. He waited until the waiter departed to continue.

"And also that slavery is illegal. The lax enforcement is what we're enjoying at the moment. That doesn't work if translators dob you in. We just can't know whether they will or not," Aron explained.

"Maybe we can find a dodgy translator that won't turn us in," Hana said with a shrug.

"Maybe. But how do we specifically find a dodgy one that doesn't respect the law but also won't be tempted by the bounty?" Aron asked.

"Ok, not dodgy; compassionate."

"Similar problem. Unfortunately, nobody advertises that they'll help you break laws when there's a noble cause."

They all stopped again to consider other options.

"Hmm... Ok, here's a plan. Maybe one of us could stay out here with Penny on the next run into home space," Hana said. "Although the downside is I guess that would have to be you. I'm guessing you will need to enter the code and whatever, being the owner."

"That would be too expensive! On top of the living costs, we'd have to hire another pilot."

"Yeah, but what other choice do we have?"

"It doesn't matter whether we have other choices," Aron said. "That's not an available option. We couldn't afford to do that, short of selling the ship."

They stopped again to reconsider the options.

"I'm sorry," Penny said.

"For what?"

"I'm causing you all this trouble!"

"It's not your fault!" Hana said forcefully.

"Definitely not your fault! You had no say in it," Aron concurred. "We're in this situation now. We just have to deal with it."

"Yeah. No point blaming anyone."

"And no one to blame. Except, maybe, Petror," Aron said with a smile.

"No! Don't blame Petror! He might have put us in this situation, but if he didn't, Penny would still be stuck as a slave!" Hana said.

"Oh. I didn't think of it like that."

There was another moment of silence before Hana decided to change the subject.

"Oh, I found a walk for us to do. Did I mention?" Hana asked.

"Yes," Aron replied.

"It's a bit of a way outside the city. I'm thinking of hiring a car."

"Is that necessary?" He asked. His tone suggested he believed the correct answer to that question was 'no'.

"Relax, I'll pay for it. Well, I'll pay you back."

"Money just comes and goes with you, doesn't it," he said.

"Well, yeah. That's what it's for," Hana laughed.

"Sometimes you have to think about the future. You know, put something aside."

"Aron, I grew up in a family with no money," Hana said shortly. "Now that I have a little, you expect me to keep living like I don't?"

Aron got defensive. "It's not crazy to save for the future."

"I know. I just want to live a little now while I can. I have plenty of time to be 'sensible' later when this venture of yours takes off, and we're all making the big bucks."

Aron sighed. "If it takes off."

"When!" Hana insisted. "Now, if you're done with your coffee, you can head back to the ship. I'm going to take Penny to Bonwe to get some of the nicer stuff to wear."

— — — — —

Very early the following morning, not long after sunrise on the Ophir Spaceport, all four of the ship's inhabitants headed to the creepers to make their way down to the planet's surface. There Hana hired a car (with Aron's money) and drove them out of Ophir City, arriving at the base of the walk just in time to see the surface's sunrise over the mountainous terrain.

"I can't believe you talked me into bushwalking," Marc said to Hana.

"It's good exercise," Aron interjected.

"It's cold. It's windy," Marc complained.

"It'll warm up when the sun gets higher," Hana said.

"Why didn't we wait until then?"

"We're going now so that Aron can join us. It's already passed his normal bedtime," Hana said. "Cheer up! Look, Penny's happy."

"These new clothes don't feel right," Penny said, frowning. "The elastic is too tight."

"Why is everyone complaining?" Hana exclaimed.

"We're bushwalking. That's what you do when bushwalking. You walk, and you complain – but in the bush," Marc said.

"No! You walk and admire nature," Hana said in a condescending tone.

"Oh, look! Rocks!" Marc said, with all the sarcasm at his command.

"I can't believe you asked him to come bushwalking!" Aron said.

"Don't you start!" Hana said.

Aron slowly looked around their surroundings as he waited for Hana to finish putting on her walking shoes. Opposite the start of the walk were fences belonging to private residences. In the distance, he could hear irregular loud bangs emanating from a nearby industrial area.

"Are you sure about this location? It doesn't seem very remote," Aron said.

"Yeah, you only hear the noises for the first minute or so, from what I've read," Hana replied.

"This is possibly the most remote place I've ever been," Penny commented.

"Oh?"

"I mean, furthest from artificial structures. At least since I was kidnapped, I've been on ships, spaceports, or the pirate's base," she explained.

"Well, it's a good thing that we brought you here. Give you a chance to experience the outdoors," Hana said, standing up.

"Yeah. I guess so," Penny said, unsure.

"You guess so?" Hana asked.

"I suppose I'm not used to being outside. It's a bit unnerving," Penny rubbed her shoulders against the wind.

"Give it a chance. I'm sure you'll love it. Now, let's go."

Hana led the way toward the start of the walk.

"If you don't like it, I'll bring you back," Marc whispered to Penny as they followed Hana.

— — — — —

Fifteen minutes into the walk, Penny had no regrets about coming. There were birds in the trees and a seemingly endless variety of both birds and trees. Every corner revealed some new wonder. Penny was thoroughly enjoying herself.

Penny and Aron were ahead of Hana and Marc, who had stopped a little way back. Marc stopped to remove a stone from his shoe, and Hana was just happy to stop for a rest. On the other hand, Penny was keen to see if the waterfall was visible from the top of the crest. Hana, to relieve her own feelings of guilt for holding Penny back, had insisted that Aron take her on ahead.

The crest had been further ahead than they thought. The steep rise had given way to a gentler slope which had made the visual distance deceptive. But Penny was almost bounding along, so Aron didn't have a chance to suggest they wait for the other two.

"There it is!" Penny exclaimed, pointing down the valley to where a narrow white ribbon draped down the wall of a cliff.

Aron took the last few steps to reach where Penny stood. "Yep, that's it."

"How far is it from here?" She asked as she took a bite from a protein bar.

"Fifteen minutes or so," he replied after checking the map. "Then we climb the steps on the far side."

They paused to look at the view for a moment.

"Uh, I'm starting to feel a little funny," Penny said. "I... I need to sit down."

Aron helped her down and seated her on the ground.

"What's the matter?" Aron asked, full of concern.

"It's —" She started.

"It's what?" Aron asked, but it was too late: Penny had already keeled over from her seated position and lay on the ground.

Aron tried briefly to wake her out of this. But as he did so, a horrible thought occurred to him. In all the excitement of being outside, they'd forgotten to key the code for the slave bolt! Perhaps Penny's lack of consciousness was a result of that!

Aron had packed the slave bolt in the bag Marc had been carrying. He was torn; should he run back and fetch it, leaving Penny alone, or wait for Hana and Marc to arrive?

He was only five steps down the hill when he saw the other two heading up. Still, he continued running until he reached them.

"What's up?" Hana asked.

"I need the bag. I forgot to do the slave bolt thing," he said hurriedly.

"I have it. What is the matter? Is Penny ok?" Hana asked as she removed the bag from her back.

"She passed out," he replied.

"Where?" Marc asked urgently.

"Just at the top, there," Aron said, unzipping the bag in Hana's grasp.

Marc ran on while Hana held the bag for Aron to rummage through.

"Where is it?" Aron asked, frustrated.

"It's in there somewhere," Hana said.

"Why do we have five umbrellas?"

"Just in case. It's definitely in there. I saw it this ... oh!" Hana went white.

"What?" Aron asked, pausing his search.

"Oh no! I think I must have left it in the car!" Hana cried.

"What? Why did you take it out?"

"I was rearranging the bag. I took everything out," she said.

"Are you sure?"

"No," she said, sounding unsure.

"Well, let's check the bag, just in case," he started pulling everything out of the bag and putting it on the ground.

"Will Penny be ok?" Hana asked, very concerned.

"I don't know. I mean, it must give you some leeway. Belike it makes the slave pass out to stop them from running away."

"You're right. That makes sense," she said, acting reassured.

"It's not here," he said.

"What do we do?"

"I'll have to go back and get it," he said. "You stay here with Marc and look after Penny."

"And what do we do if something happens?"

"I don't know," Aron called back, already cantering back down the hill.

His pace picked up as he ran down the hill and ran until he couldn't run anymore. Then he walked at a quick pace until he'd recovered a bit and started running again. He continued in this fashion all the way back down the path. By the time he had reached the start point, he was exhausted.

But he couldn't stop.

Once he reached the car, he very quickly found the slave bolt. He keyed the code into it, just in case it worked despite the distance. Then he began to make his way back.

He keyed in the code several times on his way back across the car park to the start of the walk. And did it again each time he stopped to get his breath back when running back to where he had left the others.

With only a hundred metres to go, Aron stopped to enter the code one more time, confident that it should work from there.

Just as he entered the last digit, he was startled by the sound of people coming down the hill towards him. He looked up and, to his horror, saw that it was a group of soldiers. Having visions of Marc and Hana already under arrest, he quickly hid the slave bolt behind his back and raised his free hand in an awkward wave.

"Morning, fellas," he said.

The soldiers completely ignored him as they ran passed him along the trail.

Aron hurried up the hill to where he'd last seen the others. But they were gone. He scanned the trees by the path, checking if they were hiding there. He called out for them using the quietest yell he could manage.

They didn't respond.

He stood there for a moment, considering things. If they hadn't been caught, they must have moved. And they can't have gone back the way they'd come because he was confident he would have seen them. Thus the only thing he could do was keep going.

He started walking down the other side of the hill towards the waterfall. He proceeded slowly now, not wanting to accidentally run passed his friends' hiding place – if indeed they were hiding. He resumed his ritual of entering the code regularly.

As he was nearing the waterfall, he was starting to doubt whether coming down the hill was the right thing to do. But just then, he heard Hana's voice over the roar of the falling water. His pace quickened, and he was relieved to see Hana, Marc, and Penny on the rocks near the water's edge. Penny was lying in the shade of a large tree.

"There you are!" Hana yelled at him, excited. "Did you put in the code? I think she's coming out of it."

"Yes, I put in the code."

"Oh, good."

Penny's arm slowly raised and went to her head. She pinched the bridge of her nose and screwed up her eyes for a moment. Then her eyes opened, and she looked around. She moved to sit up, but Marc held her shoulder down.

"Just rest," said Marc.

"Are you ok?" Aron asked.

She nodded weakly in reply but didn't say anything.

"Sorry! Sorry! Sorry!" Hana exclaimed. "This was my fault; I'm sorry!"

Penny waved dismissively.

"Here, have some water," Marc said, handing it to a silently grateful Penny. She lifted her head slightly to drink.

"Can you talk?" Aron asked.

"Yes," she replied weakly.

"Let's let her rest," Marc said. "She's not 100% back yet."

Aron and Marc helped Penny move so she could sit with her back against a smooth tree.

"Why did you guys move? I was worried," Aron asked.

"Marc figured people would be nosey if we had a passed-out girl on the trail at the top of the hill. But by the water, they wouldn't think anything of it. You know, she's probably just having a nap," Hana explained.

"How did you get her down here?" Aron asked.

"Marc carried her down on his back," Hana replied, miming the action.

"Good thing she's shorter than I am," Marc said.

"Ok. Good thinking, Marc," Aron said quietly.

"I was going to come back up the hill, but when the soldiers passed, I decided it would be better to wait down here a bit," Marc said.

"It's because I was freaking out," Hana admitted.

She had barely taken her eyes off Penny. Penny's eyes were closed again, taking deep, slow breaths.

Aron noticed this. "Penny, are you ok?" He asked.

"Getting better, slowly," she quietly responded.

"That's good."

"Sorry!" Hana exclaimed.

"It's my fault," Aron said.

"No, you packed the thing. I screwed up."

"Now, now! You can both be to blame," Marc laughed.

"Fine. But this can't happen again. I'm going to figure out some way to keep this on me at all times. And Penny stays with me."

"That seems a bit of an overreaction!" Hana exclaimed.

"Besides, we spend almost all of our time on the ship. Where's she going to go?" Marc added.

"I don't know. It's just bad. I don't want it to happen again."

"It won't. We'll help you," Marc said.

"Speaking of help, I think we ought to help Penny out of here," Hana said.

"Should we take her to the hospital?" Aron asked.

No one responded straight away. No one wanted to be the person who said 'no', but at the same time, they couldn't say yes.

"Don't," Penny said weakly. "They might find the slave bolt."

"Let's take her to the ship and see how she is then," Marc said.

"Penny, are you right to move? Or would you like to rest a little more?" Hana asked.

"I'm good to go," she said, standing up.

A wave of dizziness hit her, and she stabilised herself against the tree she'd been sitting against.

"Take it slowly," Marc said. "You stood up too fast."

"Yeah. Slow," Penny repeated slowly.

— — — — —

They slowly made their way to the start of the trail and then back to the ship. They filled Penny with fluids and food and then put her to bed.

"I'm going to check the cargo," Marc said.

"We don't have any yet," Aron said. "That's tomorrow, remember?"

"Oh, right," Marc said, sitting down.

"I'm such an idiot!" Hana said suddenly, surprising Aron and Marc.

"Well, I'm not going to argue with that," Marc said. "But do we know that is the cause of Penny fainting?"

"What else could it be?" Hana asked.

"Dehydration," Marc stated. "Seriously, if you go on a bushwalk and don't drink enough fluids, you faint."

"It could have been dehydration. It could even have been something else. But we still neglected the one duty we had to do."

"Yeah," Marc said. Then he turned to Aron and said, "Speaking of duty, go get some sleep. The cargo is coming tomorrow, and you know the Captain doesn't like people missing the start of their shifts."

"Yes, boss!" Aron said. He grabbed a drink, then made his way back to the bedroom and climbed into his bunk.

Time to go!
No, the kids stay here.
They come with us, or we stay with them!

Stay here. I'll talk with the transport's captain.
Oh no!
Come now.
This is where you'll be sleeping while you're with us.

Episode IV. Prar and Prejudices

"I'm tired," Hana groaned.

"So sleep. The ship's all loaded; nothing more you need to do," Aron said, heading to the ship's controls.

Hana groaned in frustration. "I don't want to sleep," she said, stamping her foot.

Aron laughed. "Well, I don't know how to help you, then," he said.

Hana looked around the ship's galley. "Where's Penny?"

"Uh, I think she's having a morning nap."

Hana quick-stepped up to the co-pilot's seat. "Do you think she hates us?" She quietly asked.

"What?" Aron asked, surprised.

"Well, we did screw up pretty bad," Hana stated.

"I don't hate you," Came Penny's voice from her bed. She slowly extricated herself from the narrow sleeping space.

"I think she's awake," Aron said. He finished what he was working on and turned the chair around.

"You're a lot more generous than I would be," Hana said. "I'd be pretty mad if Aron had done that to me."

"What? It's all my fault now?" Aron reacted with feigned shock.

"Yep. Keep with the program." Hana winked at him.

"I won't say I wasn't upset that it happened," Penny said thoughtfully. "But I can't be mad at you guys. You really want to help me."

"Too right we do," Aron said quietly. He gave Penny a friendly smile.

"We should contact Hahaha," Hana said. "He might be able to help us free her from that. He knows a few languages; I think Tungolese might be one of them."

"It's called Tun," Aron said.

"What?" Hana asked, unsure of the context.

"It's called Tun," Aron repeated deliberately and dramatically, annunciating each word.

"You named the thing?" Hana screwed up her nose at Aron.

Penny laughed. "No, he means the language is called Tun, not Tungolese."

"Oh." Hana blushed. Then she playfully punched Aron in the arm. "Since when do *you* know so much?"

"Since Penny told me," he said, rubbing his arm.

"Ah, well, that explains everything. Girls are the smartest."

Aron ignored that comment. "We'll call Hahaha once we're in Tuanti space."

"Even if he doesn't know *Tun*, he might know someone who can read that thing. He knows everyone," Hana added.

"But we don't need to worry about that until we need to make another run into Tuanti space."

"Which won't be long," Hana said. "We have to go home sometime."

"Yes, but I plan to put that off as long as possible. It'll take us twenty days to get to Dwanty. Once there, we should be able to get plenty of jobs which stay amongst the planets in the Fandusent Cluster, even if we exclude Tungol."

"Why are you excluding Tungol?" Hana asked, puzzled.

"Firstly, I don't want to take Penny back there."

"Fair," Hana said.

Penny shook her head. "You don't need to avoid it on my account," she said.

"Well, even so, my second reason is that I have this paranoid fear that someone is going to give me *another* slave. Or, at least, something else that could cause me trouble," Aron said.

"That's just typical of you! You have one bad experience and develop a paranoid fear about it happening again!" Hana said playfully.

"Shut up," Aron said, embarrassed.

Hana gave Aron a giant, cheesy smile to celebrate her triumph of wit. Aron uncharacteristically stuck his tongue out in reply. (It was what Hana would have done had the circumstances been reversed. Nevertheless, he was careful not to let Penny see him do it.)

"Aron," Penny piped up.

"Yes?"

"I've been thinking. I need something to do. I'm not used to being idle," Penny spoke quietly, intently looking at her hands as she did.

"Ok. I'm sure we could find something. Did you have anything in mind?"

"I can do anything you need!" Penny said, shaking her head in the Tungolese expression of emphasis. "One of the things I did for Petror was balance his books. I mean, he showed me what needed to be done; I just did all the maths."

"Did the pirates teach you maths?" Hana asked. "I'm picturing a man with a beard, parrot, and wooden leg teaching a class."

"Not so much," Penny laughed. "I think I was already reading a bit when they took me. But Bill helped me with my reading and basic math after we were taken. I raided the slavers' dump for reading material. The slavers dumped anything they stole that they couldn't sell and didn't want themselves. I occasionally found books and rescued them before they were disposed of. One day I found a bunch of school books in the pile. The great thing about those is that the slavers thought I would find them boring. So they never confiscated them, unlike other books."

"Once again, one of Penny's childhood stories makes me think much more positively about my upbringing," Hana said.

"I used to say the same about your stories," Aron said. "I hate to think of the person who would make Penny say that."

— — — — —

As per the schedule, they arrived in Dwanty on the twentieth day, with Hana and Marc docking the ship. They were met at the dock by the client who had requested the transport. By the time Aron woke up, the entire shipment was already gone.

"The buyer has left with all the cargo," Hana said. "I hope you didn't need her for anything."

"That's fine; it was all pre-organised."

"What are you doing?" Hana asked.

"Trying to find some new cargo for us to take. There are not as many options going out of Dwanty as I'd been led to believe."

"I thought you found some pre-booked jobs the other day?" She asked, surprised.

"They were all going into the Tuanti. I'm trying to avoid those jobs for now."

"Fair enow. I suppose it makes sense that the only companies using the Tuanti pre-book systems would be those sending stuff to the Tuanti. But I'm not sure what you expect to change between now and later when we have to go back."

"Belike nothing will change," Aron admitted. "But I'm hoping to think of some way to mitigate the risks."

"So you haven't found anything?"

"Not anything good."

"Oh! So we might have time here?" Hana asked, her excitement rising. "I'm going to look up things to do!"

"Or you could help me find some cargo!"

"No, you'll find something," Hana said, digging into her tablet.

"I'll help you, Aron," Penny said, emerging from the bedroom. "Just show me where to look."

"You don't want to eat first?" Hana asked.

"No, I'm good," She replied.

"Here, grab a console. This is Dwanty's central registry. We want cargo that is 3,000 S.C.U. or less – that's volume – and 78,000 R.T. or less – that's weight. It can't be greater than either of those values. But the closer it is, the better. Just check with me when you find something, and I'll have a look."

"Ooh, there's this!" Hana exclaimed rather loudly.

"Keep it down; Marc's asleep! What did you find?"

"It's called the Ama'ik Blowhole. It can shoot sea water over 30m into the air! It's about half a day's drive from the base of the creeper. We'd probably need to stay somewhere."

"Ok. I'm going to keep looking for cargo," Aron said. But then he stopped to add, "You shouldn't go out of your way for a blowhole. They can be pretty disappointing if the wind isn't exactly right."

"Ah, good point!" Hana said.

There were a few moments of quiet as the three concentrated on their individual research.

"What about this?" Penny asked. "The listing has more cargo than you said. But it's not a single trip; it's multiple trips."

"I don't know," Aron said. "Those jobs rarely pay enough to cover the costs of the dead-run back. And they make it difficult to find cargo to fill the ship on the way back."

"No, this has goods being moved both ways. It's a company moving goods backwards and forwards. They need to replace their previous transport company."

"Oh. Let me have a better look," Aron turned to look at Penny's console. "It can start tomorrow, which is good. The payment is just for the transport; I'd prefer it if it paid a little more."

Aron stopped to think about it further.

"I think I'll keep looking," he finally said. "They want multiple ships, so it's not likely to disappear any time soon. Let's keep that as a backup plan."

"Oh, good." Hana exhaled in relief. "I can keep looking."

"Don't get your hopes up," Aron stated.

— — — — —

Aron and Penny were still trying to lock in some cargo when Marc woke up hours later. At this point, they had found some leads and were calling around to talk to potential clients.

"Nope. That's another one where they've already booked someone," Aron said.

"How long are you intending to stay out here?" Marc asked.

"As long as I need," Aron said.

"You might be happy enough staying out here indefinitely. But I will want to go back to Tuanti space soon. And at some point, so will Hana."

"I know. But if I can hold on out here for a little while, perhaps something will come up that could help Penny."

"Perhaps. But you'll keep having trouble finding jobs that will pay well enough out here," Marc said. "You might as well just take a job heading back into the Tuanti now and look for your miracle there."

"We still have four more potential leads, not counting our fall-back plan," Aron replied. "It's a good thing we've got Penny. There are a few clients here who speak Tun. Probably not surprising, given the short distance from there to here."

Penny finished her call and joined the conversation. "That one's a no-go. They won't budge on the payment."

"Oh, that's weird," Aron said, screwing up his face. "Still, we should get one of the last three."

"Well, it's your call, big brother. But you know my opinion."

"Yeah, I do."

Aron and Marc exchanged a silent look.

"Alright, then," Marc said, heading back towards the bedroom.

"Let's move on to the next call, Penny," Aron said.

Penny was already dialling.

"Musin. Sem pers English pur Tun?" Penny said to the phone.

"Kra gas **gat** spedat rins prar-fent!" The person shouted loud enough for Aron to hear before ending the call.

"Well, that was rude! At least, it sounded rude," Aron said. He took the phone off Penny and stared at it as if it would give him some clue about what had happened.

"It was very rude. And also strange," Penny said, furrowing her brow. "He told me he won't take calls from female slaves and hung up."

"How did he even know?" Aron asked, shocked. "What exactly did you say?"

Penny shrugged. "I just greeted him and asked if he spoke Tun."

"That is strange. Maybe he thought you were someone else," he paused just a moment to consider this. "Oh well, let's try the other two and then come back to that one."

Aron and Penny had no luck with either of the other two leads. Aron called the other person back, but they didn't even answer the call. So, reluctantly, Aron decided to go with his fall-back plan.

Aron made the call this time. The client spoke English, but not a huge amount. Fortunately, they had employees who did speak English, and a deal was struck with ease. The client was desperate for transport ships due to their previous shipping contractor needing to pull out. (The official reason was just unforeseen circumstances. But the employee Aron spoke to at the client, Altur, believed the shipping company had been grounded by the Dwanty regulators for safety violations.)

"Well, it's organised. We can tell Marc and Hana to prepare for cargo mid-day tomorrow," Aron said.

"Hana might be disappointed. She was quite excited about some of the activities she found."

"Well, that can't be helped. She'll get over it quickly," Aron said. "But it's weird that we had so much trouble. Normally you get at least one of the higher-paying jobs. And I thought it would be easier when we had someone who spoke the language."

"Maybe it was because I was speaking Tun. Belike there's something about my accent or manner of speaking that gives away the fact that I was a slave."

Aron sighed. "Oh well. No use worrying about it now. At least we have something."

— — — — —

Their new job would see them spending almost two months running cargo to and from Errone, a 51-hour flight from Dwanty. The irregular flight time meant that the docking, unloading, and disembarking tasks were evenly spread amongst the crew. It also allowed them time to do some of the shorter activities Hana had found on Dwanty and Errone in between runs. Even if it didn't pay as much as Aron might have liked, the consistent work was a nice change.

All this time, Penny helped Aron to do the bookwork. One day he came to her while she was running some numbers. He handed her an envelope.

"What's this?" Penny asked.

"Your first paycheck!" Aron said with a smile.

"What?"

"You're free, Penny. Which means if you do work, you get paid."

"Am I getting paid?" Hana asked.

"Er... in a couple of days."

"Typical."

"You don't need to do this," Penny said.

"Actually, I do. It's the law; you can't have people working for you and not pay them. In any case, you don't have bank accounts or anything, so this is just cash. But that's not a good long-term solution. So I think I'll create a sub-account of the business accounts and pay into that. Then we'll look into getting your own accounts once we're in the Tuanti."

"Ok, fine. What do I owe you for the clothes? Also food and board."

"Uh. I don't know," Aron said, entirely unprepared for this question.

"It's ok; I can probably work out most of it from the books. I'll pay you back," Penny said.

Aron looked questioningly at Hana, but she just shrugged.

"Ok," Aron said slowly. "You know... there's no rush for you to pay me back, right?"

"I know. And I thank you for your generous loans," Penny said with a smile.

"Ok," Aron said again, unsure whether he should say anything else.

Hana quietly signalled for Aron to go up and take the controls. Then she went back to Penny.

"Penny, you know you can be slightly selfish with this money. It's your *first* paycheck."

Penny sighed. "I know you guys think the money thing is a big deal. And I get it. It just... doesn't mean much to me. I don't even have anything I want to spend it on. I'm not saying I'm not grateful. But all the other stuff you guys do for me means much more."

"What else do we do?" Aron asked.

"You all do a lot of little things. Aron, you make me do things for myself. Hana, you look out for me. Marc is patient with helping me learn stuff. And you all make me feel special."

"Well, that's good," Hana said. "But keep that paycheck. Pay Aron back with your next one."

"Ok. I'll do that," Penny said. Hana couldn't resist; she gave Penny a hug.

"Hey, Hana!" Aron called.

"What?"

"Hug on your off time. This is still your shift," Aron said with a smile.

"Yes, boss!" Hana sighed.

— — — — —

The two months of work seemed to pass quite quickly. But it eventually came to an end.

"What are we going to do next?" Hana asked as they unloaded the last of the cargo on Errone.

"Altur, the contact at our client, says there should be a lot of profitable work on Reude Heereen at this time of year."

"Isn't that on the far side of the Tuanti?"

"No, that's Rhyne Hearesth. Reude Heereen is about four days from here. Altur helped me organise a small payload from here to there."

"That's nice of him."

"Altur is a woman."

"Oh. I keep thinking she's a man because it sounds like Arthur. It's weird that you've had all this contact with her but never seen her. Isn't it?"

"It's not that weird. She just organised the transport. She's not going to come out here to load them. I'm going to go call her and let her know we're docked."

The last of the cargo left the ship and landed in the holding area just as the client's local transport team arrived to collect it. Altur came with them and headed over to meet them.

"Hello," she said.

"Hello. We were just talking about how we hadn't seen you," Aron said.

"I came to see you for this last load. Also, to thank you for good work you do."

"Well, it's been nice working with you."

"And you."

"You're English is very good. Do you do much business with the Tuanti?"

"Yes, yes. We do many transports to and from Tuanti. Also, in Fandusent Cluster. We do work on Dwanty, Errone, Tungol, Burdès, and Kaudes."

"Do you speak any other languages?"

"Yes. I speak Lon and Relan from Dwanty, Twaitwe from Burdès, Mio from Kaudes, and Tun from Tungol." Altur counted the languages on her fingers to ensure she didn't forget any.

"Wow. So many languages!"

"It is very useful to me," she smiled.

"I'll bet." Then an idea came to Aron. "Say, since you know Tun, can you answer a question?"

"I can only try."

"I have a friend who speaks Tun. But anytime she speaks it, people think she's a slave. Would you know why?"

Altur suddenly looked uncomfortable. "I cannot say. I would not know. But if this is case, perhaps she should not speak. People in this area do not like talking to slaves."

"But she's not a slave," Aron said.

"I cannot say," Altur said, raising and lowering her hands.

Aron decided it was best to drop the matter. They chatted amicably while the cargo was checked, and Altur bid them farewell.

"Well, that was weird, the way she just refused to talk about the slave stuff," Hana said.

"You thought so too, huh?" Aron asked.

"Absolutely. As soon as you said the word 'slave', she looked uncomfortable."

"I don't get it. Dwanty and Errone are slave-holding planets. They can't object to the practice, can they?"

Hana shrugged. "I suppose some people could."

"But why would they take it out on the slave?" Aron asked.

"Or perhaps it's not slavery they dislike; maybe they just don't want to deal with someone else's slave instead of the owner."

"That could be right. She did say that people don't like talking to slaves," Aron said.

"Well, until we figure out how they know, perhaps Penny should stop speaking Tun to clients," Hana said.

"Yeah. It's a shame; it could really come in handy."

The cargo for Reude Heereen came mere minutes after the last container of their last load had left. Since it was a small load, it was moved onboard the ship very quickly. With clearance from the Errone Spaceport's flight control, they were on their way again.

— — — — —

Four days later, they arrived at the Reude Heereen Spaceport. As they were scheduled to arrive in the middle of Aron's scheduled night, he had instructed Marc and Hana to dock the ship, see to the cargo being unloaded, and then start looking for the rumoured high-paying jobs. He had even turned in early to maximise the amount of sleep he would get in the event that he needed to be woken up.

Docking and unloading proceeded without a hitch. But the cargo hunt came with an unexpected challenge, so they deferred until Aron awoke.

"What's the issue?" Aron asked.

"It's similar to Dwanty. The Tuanti jobs go through the pre-booking system. Other jobs don't. But Reude Heereen has a central booking agency."

"So?"

"They don't speak English, and they don't have English translators. At least, that's the impression I got from my attempt at talking to them on the phone," Marc said.

Aron screwed up his face as he considered this problem.

"What's the language spoken here?" He asked.

"Nitheen," Hana said.

Aron nodded pensively. "I'm going to look up a phrase book. When Penny wakes up, I'll take her to the booking office and try to sort this out in person."

Marc and Hana exchanged a glance.

"Do you think it's wise to take Penny?" Marc asked.

"I'm not intending for her to speak. I'm hoping that I can learn enough Niseen —"

"Nitheen," Hana corrected.

"— Nitheen to ask for a translator. And if that fails, maybe she'll overhear something in Tun that will help."

"That's a big if," Marc said.

"It is. Absolute last resort, I'll get her to only say the bare minimum to ask for a translator."

"Perhaps you might consider taking one of the Tuanti jobs?" Marc quietly suggested.

"I'm not ready for that yet."

"Well, I'm going to turn in," Marc said. "Just remember, we have to go home sometime. We can't stay out here forever."

"I know," Aron said quietly.

Penny slept for a few more hours. Whilst waiting, Aron made good use of his time learning a small number of Nitheen phrases he thought might come in handy. Aron practised saying a few things to Hana. When he was confident with those, he got Hana to read a few phrases he thought someone might say to him.

By the time Penny had finished breakfast, he felt ready to head into the office.

One thing Aron hadn't considered was how to find his way to the booking office. He had assumed it would be in the docks; and had 'bunt fur', the Nitheen name of the office, written on a piece of paper in the local script to help him recognise the sign. But none of the offices at the docks matched what was written. Fortunately, someone from the crew of a departing Tuanti ship saw the two humans looking lost and gave Aron directions. Unfortunately, Aron and Penny misunderstood one of the directions and took a wrong turn. With a bit of luck, a local realised they were lost and, having seen Aron's paper, guided them to the right place.

Once inside, they followed signs to an information desk. There Aron flexed his recently acquired Nitheen. "Pumpens. English baz plenast?"

This was close enough that the man behind the information desk guided Aron and Penny to the only person in the office who spoke English.

"Pumpens. Hello. My name is Trufis. I am one booking agent here. Can I help you?" The lady said with the largest smile Aron had seen.

"Pumpens. My name is Aron, and this is Penny. We're looking to book some cargo."

"Are you going somewhere spacifically?"

"No. Anywhere is fine."

Trufis stopped and took another look at Penny. "You look familiar," she said. "Have you been in here before?"

"No," Penny said quietly.

Aron turned to look at her and noticed a look of panic on her face.

"I am very sure that I will remember you. I have never forgotten someone's face," Trufis said with a smile.

Trufis returned to her computer, took the name and capacity of Aron's ship, and started looking up available jobs. But then it occurred to her how she knew Penny.

"That is Petror's slave! I saw it on Tungol Spaceport!" She said to Aron. "You do not need to introduce a slave."

Trufis started looking at her computer again, but Aron was annoyed.

"Penny is not a slave; she is a person," he said calmly but with force. He immediately knew this had been the wrong thing to say.

Trufis' smile was gone. "People say: you cannot get bronze from dirt. Perhaps humans have been in the stars too long to remember."

Aron couldn't believe what he had heard. "What?" He shouted. "Where do you think bronze comes from?"

"You do not know how things are," Trufis said bluntly, raising and lowering her hand in a dismissive sign.

"You don't seem to know basic compassion."

Trufis wasn't going to put up with this. "You must leave," she said loudly and forcefully.

"Hold on; I need cargo," Aron said, hoping Trufis might value professionalism enough to allow him to get cargo despite their disagreement.

"Your ship will not get any cargo on this spaceport. I will ensure!"

Aron glared at her for a moment. She glared back with twice the ferocity.

"Let's go, Penny."

He stormed out. Penny followed meekly behind.

Aron quietly stomped all the way back to the ship. His abrupt entry startled Hana.

"What happened?" She asked in shock.

"Still too angry!" Aron said. "We're leaving."

"What about the cargo?"

"There is none," he said. Then he pointed at Penny to ask her to explain. He flopped into the pilot's chair before stopping himself and taking a moment to breathe.

Penny was still in shock. But she was gathered enough to speak. "The booking agent had visited Petror on Tungol. She remembered me. And when Aron told her I was free, she refused to serve us. She said she would block our ship from getting any cargo here."

"Why would you tell her that?" Hana asked a bit too loudly.

"She was being disrespectful! Ah... I knew it was the wrong thing to say as soon as I said it," Aron said.

The moment's passion was starting to cool, and he was beginning to realise what a predicament he'd gotten himself into.

"Without cargo, we'll need to make a dead-run." He let out a loud sigh. "That's going to cost me so much money!"

"Perhaps we can go back and apologise?" Hana suggested.

Aron reacted indignantly. "No chance of that happening. I'm not going back there."

Hana didn't know what to say. She flopped herself down in the co-pilot's seat.

"What's the nearest planet?" Aron asked, his voice as calm and controlled as he could force it to be.

Hana looked it up. "Dhen. It's a recently settled planet. Its spaceport only opened last year."

"We'll go there and take whatever we can find," Aron said, already starting to prepare the ship. "Unless you can suggest a better plan. Clearly, my judgement is off today."

"No, I think you're right. Let's leave this maggot-hole behind," Hana said.

Aron and Hana cleared with the port authority and took the ship out of the dock. Once they were in the space corridor to Dhen, Aron handed control to Hana.

"I need a break," he said. "I got too wound up."

"Fair enough," Hana said. "I've got this."

"I'm sorry about all of that, Penny," Aron said, sitting on a galley seat next to Penny.

"It's not your fault. I'm sorry for costing you a cargo."

"Don't worry about the cargo; that was not your fault. Not in any way. And I'm not apologising for that scunner. She can go rot for all I care. I'm sorry for speaking on your behalf. I shouldn't have done that."

"I don't mind. I don't really know how to react to those situations."

"Well, I've shown you how *I* react; that's for sure. I'm not sure that's a good example to follow, though."

Aron stood up and headed toward the back of the ship.

"I'm going to go find something to throw at something in my vast, empty hold. That should calm me down," he said.

He disappeared through the bedroom door, closing it behind him.

"Penny. Come sit," Hana said.

"Is he alright?" Penny asked, sitting in the co-pilot's seat.

"He'll be fine. How are you?"

"I'm fine. I'm fain."

"Are you?" Hana asked seriously.

"Yeah. It was a bit of a rush. I thought they might physically throw Aron out at one point."

"I can imagine. But Aron doesn't get angry like that often. It must have been something serious. Are you sure you're alright?"

"Well, yeah," Penny said. "I guess I'm used to people treating me like that."

"Ah. In that case, I hope one day you become unused to it. Maybe we can help you learn to stand up for yourself a bit. But in the meantime, if you need anything or are upset, you let me know."

"Of course."

"Now, let's take our mind off of that. Why don't we play I-spy."

"Ok, I spy with my little eye something beginning with 'S'," Penny said.

"Stars," Hana guessed.

"Correct."

"Well, my one also starts with 'S'."

"Space," Penny guessed.

"Correct. Isn't this fun!" Hana laughed.

Get 'em done, girl!
Here, I'll help with those.
Thanks, Bill. You're always making things easier for me.
Bill, come.
Penny, I need you to clean inside all those cupboards.

Where's Bill?
Gone with the last shipment.

Episode V. Pesky Police

"I miss my dad!" Hana groaned.

Her performance this time was dramatic and spotless. But Aron was distracted by his bookkeeping, and it took him a moment to register that Hana had even said something. (That moment was about how long it took Hana to realise, turn around, and poke him.)

"Hold on, Hana; sorry," Aron said. "Penny, I think Petror gave us less money than I expected. Look."

Penny ignored the numbers Aron was trying to show her. "Where's the paperwork he gave you?"

Aron pulled it up on the screen.

"Can you read this?" Aron asked.

"Not really, just the numbers."

Penny studied the pages for a few moments.

"Ok, look here," she said, pointing at what she found. "Petror has subtracted a fraction of 100 Drax from the payment. 100 Drax is what he originally bought me for. That's where your missing money is."

"What do you mean?" Aron asked, not following.

"He subtracted 44 Drax from the payment he gave you, right? That's about four-ninths of my value as a slave, based on what he paid for me."

Aron understood the words but not the reasoning. "Why did he do that? I thought he said you were a gift!"

"Oh! It's not really a gift. It's a thoughtful payment," Penny explained.

Aron had never heard of such a thing. "A what?" He asked.

Penny to a moment to prepare herself for the explanation. "On Tungol, they have these concepts of 'thoughtful gifts' and 'thoughtful payments'. If someone makes a mistake that costs someone else money, they must make some amends. But you are supposed to choose something that shows that you're sorry, something you have actually put thought into. That's called a 'thoughtful gift'. But they also have rules saying that you can use four-ninths of that gift's value as part of any restitution or other transaction. When you do that, it becomes a 'thoughtful payment'. Does that make sense?"

"I'm not sure if it makes sense, but I followed what you were saying," Aron said.

"It's a big deal on Tungol; you can get into trouble if you don't give someone a thoughtful payment when you're supposed to. But at the same time, a lot of bad stuff goes with it. Petror complained that people use them as bribes; they'll make a tiny mistake and use that as an excuse to give a thoughtful payment to whomever they want to bribe. But what Petror does is also bad; he uses it to get rid of things that would normally sell for less than the four-ninths value."

"Wouldn't you would have sold for more?" Hana asked. "I thought someone said slaves sold for 200 Drax."

"Belike I would have. Slaves were selling cheap when Petror bought me, from what I heard. But I was costing him money in food and wasn't producing baby slaves. I guess Petror just decided I was the easiest thing for him to give away. He always said he was happy with the work I did."

Aron sighed. "Anyway, the upshot is that we made about twenty-two hundred credits less than I thought that run."

"Sorry," Penny apologised.

"No, no. Let's call that a fair price for your freedom. I just wasn't expecting it."

"Shouldn't you have figured that out a long time ago?" Hana asked accusingly.

"I've been procrastinating," Aron explained. "Nobody makes you do the numbers when you're outside Tuanti space."

Aron stared at the numbers again. He hoped he'd find something good in them to make him feel better. But while the numbers weren't bad, there wasn't anything particularly good about them either. Their work in the Fandusent Cluster was paying just well enough. But they certainly could be doing better if they worked across the Tuanti border.

"Sorry, Hana. What were you saying before?" He asked.

"I want to go home," Hana said simply.

"I know. I do, too," Aron replied. "I didn't anticipate how bad the homesickness would get. And it's only been three months since we were home!"

"Three? It feels like a year! I think even Penny must be sick of this. Right Penny?" Hana asked.

"Don't ask me. I don't have a home to miss. And I quite like what we're doing. We get to see all sorts of new places. Plus, I saw an actual sheep on Dhen," Penny stated.

"They were dhenese caprids, but close enough. I'm glad someone is enjoying our tour of the universe's docks and warehouses," Aron laughed.

Hana just glared at Aron with an unimpressed expression.

"Can we go home now? Please?" She asked pleadingly.

Aron considered his response. "It's still risky," he said. "But after this run, I think we should try our luck and go home."

"Finally!" Hana said, oozing relief. "I never want to go on such a long work trip again."

"It had to be soon, anyway. We need to resupply. Plus, my hair is getting into my eyes."

"I could cut your hair," Hana said.

Aron considered this for a moment.

"We could try that," Aron said. "Anyway, we're almost close enough to Flaase to start looking for Tuanti-bound jobs. Hopefully, I can find one ready for when we arrive tomorrow."

"Shouldn't be too difficult, I think," Hana said.

"No, it shouldn't. So far, all these planets have had some good jobs going into the Tuanti," Aron said. "But we still have to think about how we can get in safely."

"Speaking of which," Marc's voice came from behind them, startling Hana.

"I thought you had gone to sleep!" She said.

"No, I've been chatting with some friends. They said the Hogian checkpoint was closed for unexpected maintenance. It's looking like it will be closed for at least a week. I mean, not officially for obvious reasons."

"What friends?" Aron asked incredulously.

"I have friends!" Marc retorted.

"No, I know you have friends! But how could they know about something like that? Especially if it's not official."

"They went that way yesterday. I think they were there when the malfunction happened. Besides, it's small, so we might get through even if it is reopened sooner."

"I don't know," Aron sighed doubtfully. "Hogian isn't a direct flight. And if it has an extended closure, belike they will send a patrol cruiser to check ships."

"A cruiser can't check even half the ships that go through a small checkpoint. I'd say it's worth a shot. And it's only a day out of the way," Hana said. "I mean, we're depending on luck anyway. This might push that luck in our favour."

"It's an extra day to get there, plus more on the other side if we're going to Angish. But I suppose you guys are right."

"What's on Hogian, anyway?" Hana asked. "I've heard the name, but I've never heard anything about it."

"I've been once," Marc said. "There's not a lot there. It wouldn't surprise me if the checkpoint was its main employer."

"I think it's mainly a military outpost," Aron said. "The only people there are military or working for things that serve the military."

"Is that risky for us, going so close to a military base?" Penny asked.

"I wouldn't think so. Why would the military care?" Marc replied.

"This might sound crazy, but how hard could it be to hide a person from an inspection," Hana asked.

"You could hide a small box easily enough," Marc said. "But Penny will need a little more space than a small box, plus fresh air to breathe."

"Withal, if they find you are hiding someone, you're bound to get into big trouble, whether they know the person is a slave or not," Aron added.

"Well, I did tell you it was crazy," Hana said quietly.

— — — — —

Aron was supposed to be asleep. But he couldn't stop worrying about what would happen when they reached the checkpoint. It was now just a matter of hours; they would arrive at the checkpoint towards the end of his next shift. Aron decided that if he was awake, he'd use the time productively, so he dug up his partially-completed financial statement.

Marc was flying the ship. Hana had woken early and was using her breakfast time to have some 'girl time' chatting with Penny.

"What do pilots do, exactly?" Penny asked. "There's nothing to hit out here. There's plenty of room for ships to pass each other. Can't ships just fly themselves?"

"Well, they do, and they don't. The ship's computers do all the work of moving the ship. The pilot's job is to monitor what is going on, make sure the computers and engines and everything are working correctly and doing the right things, and correct any problem that might occur. Perhaps 'engineer' is a better job title, though."

"Fair enow," Penny said.

"Withal, there might not be much to do when you're in the middle of nowhere, but things can get pretty hectic docking and departing a port. That's when things are most likely to go wrong. And if something does go wrong, that's where they can cause the biggest problems."

"What kind of things go wrong?" Penny asked.

Hana shifted her position to prepare herself for a long tale. "One time, a passenger ship had a thrust sensor fail when it was trying to leave the Greenwood Spaceport above Weal. The ship thought it was producing more thrust from one jet than it actually was. Since it wasn't producing enow thrust and was so close to the planet, it immediately dived. It was only by good luck that it missed the orbital ring. Now **that** would have been disastrous! If it had managed to sever the ring, it would have taken down all of the spaceports on that ring; and Weal is the most populated planet in the Tuanti. Oh, but good news: the ship, and everybody aboard, survived. The pilots figured out what was happening before it hit the atmosphere."

Penny was shocked. "If it's so easy to take down the orbital rings, that sounds like an accident waiting to happen!"

Hana waved her hand dismissively. "This was years ago. They mandate redundant rings on all Tuanti spaceports these days. Taking out a ring might still be bad news, but it's not catastrophic. Tungol only has a single ring, I hear. Beadful has three in a cross-ring design, which is unusual. One goes east-to-west, one goes west-to-east, one goes north-south."

"Wow," Penny said quietly. She looked at Hana. "You know a lot about space stations!"

"Not really. I learned about the legal stuff as part of a class assignment. The ring information is part of standard docking information. And the Greenwood Spaceport incident I learnt about from a TV show."

"There's a TV show about near-misses?" Penny asked.

"No, it's about investigating what caused crashes. But occasionally, they show near-misses as well," Hana explained.

"That sounds, well, not that interesting," Penny laughed.

"No! It's good! Here, I'll show it to you."

"Please don't," Aron interjected.

"What? Why not?"

"I'm still trying to do the finances. I'm having enough trouble concentrating on it as it is," Aron explained.

Hana was about to say something, but Penny spoke first.

"Let me help you with that," Penny said.

"Ok," Aron said.

"No! Not now," Hana said firmly. "Aron, you're always nagging us to sleep at the right time; now it's my turn to tell you. Go sleep!"

Aron thought about protesting (it was actually a little before his sleep time). But he decided against it. "You're right; I should sleep," he sighed.

He started to tidy up what he was working on.

"It can be hard to keep to the work schedule on a ship," Hana said. "You're going to sleep when someone else is waking up, and someone else is in the middle of their day. And the lights are always on, so there's no daylight cycle to help your body."

"It's not easier without a fixed schedule. My body doesn't know what to do," Penny said.

"Yeah. Not much you can do about it." Hana shrugged. "I've heard of four-person crews working in pairs, and each pair has the same wake-up and sleep times. I'm not sure I'd like that. At least with the three-person rotation, you work with everybody."

As soon as Aron had stowed his work safely, he shuffled back to the bedroom. He changed in the bathroom and then slumped himself into his bed. He didn't slide the cover down; subconsciously, he wanted to be able to hear every noise in case the checkpoint authorities came knocking.

As for how things would play out, Aron was having trouble relaxing. His mind kept going back and forth. One minute it was expecting something would go disastrously wrong. The next minute he'd convince himself that nothing would happen and all will be well. He started thinking of possible ways of explaining how Penny came to be on board his ship, with no identification papers, no destination, and without even a full name.

"Hana, Penny!" He called out.

"Yes?" Hana asked, putting her head through the bedroom door.

"Why don't you guys brainstorm a backstory for Penny? You know, in case we're asked," Aron suggested.

Hana clapped her hands together. "Oh, that might be fun! What do you want to be, Penny?"

"I don't know," Penny replied.

"What about a millionaire heiress?" Hana suggested.

"What do they do?" Penny asked.

"Nothing. They inherit a lot of money when their parents die."

"And why would I be on this ship if I had all that money?"

Hana was stumped for a second. "Uh. Perhaps you're trying to escape from —"

"Hana! Don't make the story ridiculous!" Aron interrupted.

"Yeah, we better keep it simple," Penny said. "How about a farmer or something? I think I'd like to live on a farm. I've only ever lived in cramped metal boxes."

"Oh, yes. That's a good idea. And you're running from—"

"Hana!" Aron cried.

"I was joking!" She laughed.

— — — — —

Possibly an hour or more later, Aron still wasn't asleep. (It was possible he had briefly slept but had awoken to his worries again.) Hana and Penny had quickly forgotten the backstory discussion. Penny had asked Hana about life on the other ships she had worked aboard. Aron had heard all of this before, but he still found Hana's colourful descriptions of the kinds of smell found aboard 'the stinker' amusing.

"Ok, my turn for a question. What are the dating prospects for a slave?" Hana asked as she combed Penny's hair.

"I can't speak for all slaves, but Mathieu was pretty much the only 'prospect' for me," Penny said dismissively.

"You weren't at all interested?" Hana asked.

Penny squirmed a little. "I don't know. We were just told to try to have kids. And neither of us wanted that to happen."

"Think of it like this, if you just met somewhere, would you consider dating him?"

"No. He only spoke French, so I could only speak to him in broken Tun. You can't have a relationship without communication," Penny said.

"Hah! I know a couple who can only talk to each other through a second language they don't know well," Hana stated.

"Does it work?" Penny asked.

"It seems to. I don't know them all that well," Hana said. "What about growing up? Were there any good-looking pirates? Or, (what was his name?) Bill?"

"Bill was more like an older brother," Penny said with a definite tone.

"Whatever happened to him?" Hana asked.

"When he was old enough, they took him aside and asked if he wanted to join their crew. He said no. So they sold him," Penny sighed.

"Oh."

Penny shook her head. "I didn't even know until after he'd gone. The Captain had deliberately timed the question for when there was a ship going out. The Captain came and asked him to help with something, then I never saw him again."

"That would have been rough," Hana said.

"Yeah, it really was. I was very close to Bill."

"Did they ever ask you that?" Hana asked, then answered her own question. "Well, I guess you said no too."

Penny shook her head.

"I was never asked," she said. "It didn't matter; one of the pirates had it in for me. When the Captain and Jor were away, he shipped me off to be sold."

"He could just do that?" Hana asked.

"Not really," Penny scoffed. "I suspect he got into trouble over that. He wasn't very bright."

"What kind of trouble could he have gotten into?"

"I don't know. It was rare for someone to be punished. And then there was a weird culture of not talking about the punishments. One might come back looking upset. Another might not come back at all."

"Maybe they sell them!" Hana laughed.

"Yeah, belike," Penny said seriously. Hana was taken aback. But she decided to change the subject.

"So not Bill. Were there ever any other kids?"

"No. The person acting as the hook, or mole, was supposed to check that there were no kids. Slavers don't want kids; they can't sell them and don't want to keep them. So they would get themselves booked into a business flight to reduce the chance of there being kids on board. For some reason, the hook either didn't check on our flight or just proceeded anyway."

"They can't just dump the kids at a port or something?"

"Too risky. Kids are noisy and attract attention. And belike they'll remember something which helps the authorities track down the pirates."

"Well, er... there is one more option."

"Pirates are scunners, but even they don't like killing people if they can avoid it. That doesn't prevent them from killing. But if they can avoid it, they will. There are exceptions, real scunners who will kill someone for fun. But those people don't last very long in a slaver crew; their crew mates won't stand for it."

"Yeah, that's not much of a redeeming factor," Hana said.

"No, you're right."

"But Aron would probably say, 'don't judge someone until you've walked in their shoes,' or something," Hana said.

Not in this instance, Aron thought. He considered shutting the cover on his bed to silence the talking. But he decided he didn't want to move from his comfortable position.

"What about kids of slaves on Tungol?" Hana asked.

"Legally, they're supposed to stay with their parents and be free when they're 17. But mostly, they go to orphanages. Sometimes the owners keep them, raise them, and sell them."

"I guess Petror was intending to keep any baby you had."

"Belike. Anyway, enough about me. What about you?" Penny asked.

"I don't have any kids!" Hana exclaimed.

"No, I mean dating."

"Ah... Let's not talk about me," Hana said.

"Come on. I shared my stories."

"It's awkward."

"And mine wasn't?"

"No. I mean, it's awkward to talk about it here."

"Why? Marc has got his music on, and Aron is asleep."

Aron heard the door slide open. He wasn't pretending to be asleep; he really was trying. The door slid closed again.

"Let's talk about something else," Hana simply said.

"What about when you were growing up?" Penny asked.

It was easy for Penny and Hana to switch to talking about teenage life on the Angish spaceport. But Aron had too much on his mind.

Eventually, however, exhaustion took over, and he slept.

— — — — —

"Marc, you take the helm," Aron called back to Marc.

"Why?" Marc asked, surprised.

"I don't want to be distracted as we approach the checkpoint," Aron explained.

"In case of what?"

"I don't know!" Aron said, frustration starting to appear in his voice. "But I'm nervous. And more importantly, I'm in charge. Take the helm."

"Fine."

"We're about ten minutes out. Traffic is starting to rise."

"Yeah, look at all this traffic. There must be ... two other ships!" Marc said, his voice dripping with sarcasm.

"Sarcasm acknowledged," Aron said with a sigh.

"Look, it'll be fine. If there is any inspection, don't give them any reason to be suspicious."

"A reason like that we've been away for four months now when our stated plan was 14 days?"

"That's not unusual for a freelance transport ship," Marc said coolly.

"Ok, well, how about the fact that we're coming in on a space lane which suggests that we could easily have gone to a larger checkpoint instead."

"Still not unusual. There's a reason this space lane exists. And they don't know our destination."

"Until we have to state it."

"Calm down, Aron. You're vexing," Marc said.

Aron was confused. "Sorry? Am I annoying you?"

"What?"

"You said I'm vexing," Aron explained.

"I think I used the wrong word. I meant you're working yourself up. The point is, there's no use worrying when we don't even know what, if anything, we need to worry about."

"Yeah, maybe."

"You'll feel better as soon as we are passed the checkpoint."

"If we pass the checkpoint—"

"Relax!" Marc insisted. "Now you're getting 'vexing'! I've hidden the slave bolt. They can't tell she's a slave without that. They are designed to be invisible to law enforcement, after all. And it's unlikely they'll look at us that closely, anyway. Even if they're open, there are *two* other ships they could choose."

"So now two is a big number?" Aron asked.

"It is in this case."

"Still so many unknowns!" Aron sighed. "Do you think we should have got a fake passport for Penny?"

"From where?"

"I don't know."

"Not much of a plan, then," Marc laughed.

They were just able to see the checkpoint now, a small bright spot distinct from the stars around it.

"We're getting the hail," Aron said. He played the message.

"This is a recorded message from the Tuanti Hogian Security Checkpoint controller. This checkpoint is closed for repairs. Please give a detailed manifest of your cargo, crew, and passengers, and make any necessary declarations before proceeding passed the checkpoint. Providing a false manifest or failing to declare a restricted cargo is an offence. Your ship's identifier has been logged, and you may be followed up for an inspection at a later date."

"They never do," Marc said.

"Well, you were right about it being closed," Aron said. "I guess we're ok."

Aron got to work preparing to send the manifest.

"Should we list Penny? And if so, how?" He asked Marc.

"List her as a passenger. You don't need to give much detail for passengers."

"Could cause problems if they ask," Aron stated.

"We could have problems if they ask anyway. That's not likely, now."

"Fair."

Aron sent off the manifest when they were still approaching the checkpoint station. They passed close enough that the ship's cameras could clearly see the checkpoint. It was visibly closed: its large navigation beacons were active, but all the other lights were off, and its hangar was empty.

"Penny!" Marc yelled back, where Penny was reading.

"Yeah?"

"Welcome to the Tuanti, our home."

"Or possibly welcome back," Aron added.

"It looks very much like the space we just left," Penny said, coming up to the front of the ship.

"It is very much like the space we just left, but a bit safer. There are regular patrols, and the borders are watched. And if you leave your space-lane in patrolled space, you better have a very good excuse," Marc said.

"Fair enow, too. There's practically no reason to leave a space lane. There's nothing out there," Aron said.

"I was just giving an example," Marc said.

"I know. Do you mind just continuing on until your shift? I'll make it up to you tomorrow," Aron said.

"It's fain. It's only a little early; don't bother making it up." Marc said.

"Thanks," Aron said.

He gave Marc a puzzled look, but Marc was already donning headphones.

"That's weird," Aron said to Penny. "Marc is usually reluctant to do extra time."

"Yeah, well, Hana told him to be a bit more understanding of how stressful being captain could be."

"Really? Was that it? Did they say anything else?" Aron asked.

"Uh, Marc suggested you should hire another pilot. And Hana said you'd never find one because of line carriages or something."

"Bulk carriage lines. They're big mass-transport ships that fly predictable routes. They're slower than smaller, point-to-point ships like ours. But they're also cheaper. And they're expanding, making it hard to compete sometimes. Especially between Tuanti planets."

"Yeah, so Hana said you wouldn't find a pilot because everyone wants to work on those ships."

"Well, she's right," Aron sighed. "They're larger ships, meaning more space and more people to interact with. I keep expecting Hana to tell me she's leaving for one of those jobs. It'd be a much better job for someone as social as Hana. Plus, they pay consistently. I don't know why she stays."

"Well, if you don't know, don't expect me to tell you," Penny said.

"How could you if we don't know?" Aron laughed.

"What about Marc?" Penny asked.

"Marc's my brother; he wouldn't ditch me. My dad would rip into him. I mean, he is allowed to leave, but my dad would make sure he helped find a replacement first."

"And what about you? Is this ship worth it?"

Aron wasn't quite ready for that question. "Uh. Yeah. I mean, running the ship has challenges I wasn't necessarily expecting. But I couldn't go back to working for someone else."

Penny sighed. "It's nice that Marc and Hana are willing to do so much to help you. I've never had anything like that. Except for Bill, but then he got taken away."

"Penny, you're mistaken." Aron smiled.

She just looked at him, puzzled.

"You've got three people wanting to do all we can to help you."

Penny smiled. "Thanks."

"Now, I'm going to have dinner. You want anything?"

"No, thanks. I'll keep reading my book," Penny said.

Aron had intended to watch something while he ate. Instead, he found himself thinking back over what he and Penny had discussed. A nagging feeling told him he'd missed something important.

— — — — —

Twenty-one hours after they had passed the checkpoint, Aron had almost forgotten the panic from the day before. He ate breakfast while Hana was up in the cockpit, quietly listening to music as she piloted the ship.

Then Hana removed her headphones and turned around.

"Uh, Aron; you might want to come up here. We're being hailed by a police cruiser," she said nervously.

Aron put his food down and hurried up to the cockpit.

"Eastern Light; this is police cruiser Munroe," a voice from the radio stated.

"This is Aron McNamara, captain of the Eastern Light; go ahead," Aron said.

"This is Officer Patrick Randall of the Munroe. We're conducting follow-up checks with ships that have entered via the Hogian Checkpoint."

"No problem," Aron said, his voice belying his internal reaction. "What do you need?"

"I'm going to ask you a series of questions to confirm your statements about what you have brought into Tuanti Space. Please confirm that you are ready and able to answer such questions."

"I am ready."

"First things, you listed a passenger by the name of Penny. Is that correct?"

"It is."

"Your ship doesn't have passenger quarters according to its registration. Is that correct?"

"It is. We're just giving the passenger a ride to Angish. She's sleeping in the crew quarters," Aron said.

"That's fine. Do you have any of the identification document details for that passenger?"

"I do not. Er... I'm not sure if she has those. Do you want me to wake her up to ask her?"

"No need. We're just doing random checks of the details you provided to the checkpoint. Now, onto the cargo."

The officer asked Aron a series of questions confirming some of the details he had included in the manifest. Usually, this requirement to repeat a bunch of tiny minutiae might have annoyed Aron. But at this moment, he was just relieved that they had skipped past the Penny issue without incident.

"Thanks for your time, Captain. I will be forwarding this information to the authorities on Angish."

"No problem."

"And just to let you know, the port authorities might ask you for further verifications when you dock at the Angish Spaceport," the officer said. "Good day."

"Good day."

Aron let out a large breath when he heard the call disconnect sound.

"Bet that call made your heart skip a few beats!" Hana said.

"No bet," Aron replied.

"So we're in the clear, it seems. They didn't seem to care all that much about checking stuff."

"That might come when we dock," Aron said.

"It might. Belike not, though. I don't think it's likely unless we have been inadvertently close to some pirate activity recently."

"Well, there are still risks. But at least we're passed the hardest one."

"Yeah, I'm already feeling the holiday mode," Hana said. "But we're still eight days from home!"

"Well, don't slack off now. The boss might get upset," Aron joked. "You know how he is."

Hana laughed. "Nah, he's a push-over."

Hey there, Diné... Deee-naaa!
Get off it, Noggs! Not tonight.
The kid's 'bout old enow now.
Don't even think about it; Cap will kill you.
But you...
Girl! Come!
I can't get 'em preggers.

No!
Don't ever refuse me, *slave*!
Hey! Come back here!
Catch her, Noggs!
Hey, *scunner*! If you ever touch her, I *will* hurt you.
If you have any more trouble like that, you let me know, and I will deal with the person most severely.
Jor,
am I really just a slave?
Everyone is a slave.
Best to talk to the Captain.

Episode VI. Presumptuous Proposition

"Why does everything cost money," Hana asked.

"Huh? What are you buying?" Aron asked.

"I wanted to buy this watch, but it's ¤300, and I don't have enow money," Hana said, pointing to a watch on her tablet computer.

"How much more do you need? I can probably help you out."

"Uh... another ¤296," Hana laughed.

"Oh. I don't have that much. Maybe after the next job."

"You always say that. And yet you never have any money."

"That's because there's always an unexpected bill that needs paying," Aron explained.

"Perhaps they shouldn't be 'unexpected' if they're always happening," Hana playfully suggested.

"Ha ha," Aron said sarcastically.

"Hey, have you noticed anything weird about Marc?" Hana asked, out of nowhere.

Aron was taken by surprise. "No. Like what?"

"It's just little things. He has been going to the cargo hold a lot and keeps talking about going home. Maybe he's just homesick."

"Maybe," Aron said, thinking.

"It's hard to tell. Marc's more closed off than you are about feelings and stuff. But you're his brother, so maybe he told you something."

"I'm the last person he'd tell **because** I'm his brother," Aron said.

"Anyway, we're getting close to home now. When do we dock?" Hana asked.

Aron responded by pointing to where he was up to on the docking checklist.

"Sorry, a bit excited. It has been a while since we were home last," Hana said.

"This would be a lot easier if you helped out a bit," Aron hinted.

"I'm going to wake Penny up!" Hana said, excitedly running off.

"Or you could wake Penny up, I suppose," Aron said quietly to himself.

Hana returned in a moment with Penny.

"You see, that's Angish! That's our home!" Hana said, gesturing to the growing orb in their front windows. Then, without a word, she sat down in the co-pilot's seat and started helping Aron with the docking checklist.

Penny gazed at the planet on the viewscreen. "It's so blue!" She exclaimed in awe.

"Yeah, it's mostly water. There's one large island, a number of smaller islands around that, and then a few that are a bit more distant. But the rest is just one large shallow ocean. More people live on the spaceport than down on the planet," Aron said.

"Only rich people live on the planet," Hana said, gesturing with her head toward Aron.

"We weren't rich!" Aron said matter-of-factly.

"Your family owns land! That makes you rich by almost any measure," Hana responded emphatically.

"My great-great-grandmother bought land here when the spaceport was still being built, so the land was cheap," Aron explained for Penny's benefit.

"Uhuh. And your family held on to it when others couldn't," Hana pointed out.

"Not all of it. Some of my relatives have sold all or part of their lots, particularly my great-uncle's side."

"I bet you guys still hold most of it. Think about how much that land would be worth now!"

"Doesn't matter," Aron said, shaking his head. "It's not like you can use your home to buy necessities! Both of my parents had to work just to give us the basics."

"What did they do?" Penny asked, earnestly wanting to know.

"My dad worked in the local supermarket—"

"Store manager," Hana interjected.

"— and my mum was an accountant."

"Someone who deals with money," Hana explained to Penny (unnecessarily).

"What about your family, Hana?" Penny asked.

"My dad works in freight. My mum disappeared. She ran off not long after I was born."

"Or was kidnapped," Aron added.

"Or just visiting relatives, or temporarily working off-world, or any of the half dozen other lies I was told," Hana said bitterly.

"That sucks," Penny said.

"Yeah. Anyway, back to the point. Dad and I lived with my uncle and aunt because none of them could afford to live somewhere on their own. We lived in a rented, tiny three-bedroom apartment with no windows. Well, not without moving to some backwater planet like Feng."

"Ok, fine. You win the 'who was poorer as a kid' competition," Aron conceded.

"Uh, I think I win that!" Penny said quietly.

"Maggots!" Hana exclaimed. "Aron, we're going to have to get rid of her. I can't lose the pity game!"

"Hey, we're getting close now!" Penny exclaimed. "Is it just me, or is that spaceport huge?"

"It is huge. Weal has more spaceports, but ours is easily the largest in the whole Tuanti."

"Yeah, but Weal has large cities on the surface. Angish just has *poor* farming villages," Aron said.

"Rich farming villages," Hana whispered.

But Aron didn't react; he was distracted by an incoming call.

"Shush. It's Hahaha," he told Hana as he moved to answer it. "Hello, Hahaha!"

"Hi, Aron!" Yahatha's voice called through the speaker.

"And Hana!" Hana announced.

"And Penny," Aron added.

"Who's Penny?" Yahatha asked, confused.

"Long story. I was trying to call you earlier," Aron said.

"Yeah, I saw that. Couldn't have responded earlier, though. But I just docked and saw your ship's approach on the radar. We need to meet up; if you have time. I have a lot to tell you."

"Yeah, that would be great!"

"Alright, I gotta finish unloading first. I'll meet you in the usual diner in half an hour or so. Say, 4am? Does that work for you?"

"Belike we'll be a few minutes late, but we'll be there."

— — — — —

Aron, Hana, and Penny were indeed a few minutes late for the rendevous. (Marc was sound asleep at this time.)

Yahatha was waiting for them when they arrived. As it was the quiet morning hours according to the spaceport's time, Yahatha was the only customer present. The diner's night-shift staff looked more annoyed than welcoming toward their patrons.

"Aron! Hana!" Yahatha said, standing up to greet them.

"So good to see you, Hahaha!" Aron replied as he and Yahatha slapped hands.

"I guess this is Penny?" Yahatha said, looking down at the girl who didn't even reach his shoulders.

"That's right. Penny, this is Yahatha; but call him Hahaha," Aron said.

"Hello," Penny squeaked.

"He makes you feel like you're Tungolese, doesn't he!" Aron said.

"Yes!"

"I'm going to show Penny what food they have," Hana said.

"Hold on!" Yahatha said, but Hana and Penny were gone. "Typical Hana."

"You know how she is," Aron said.

"Yeah," Yahatha chuckled. "How are you guys?"

"Well. Work is a bit relentless. Perils of running your own ship, I suppose."

"It's no better working for someone else," Yahatha sighed. "But on a small ship like yours, are you guys driving each other crazy?"

"No. Well, Marc drives everyone crazy, at least sometimes. But aside from that, it's alright."

"How long are you in port for this time?" Yahatha asked.

"The plan is to stay a week for some well-earned time off. We've been away for months. I'll put the ship in cold storage and go down to the planet to stay with my parents for some of it. Need to save some money. What about you?"

"We'll be grounded for at least a few days waiting on some repairs, it looks like. The XO thinks it will be two weeks at least. Although the Captain will probably blow a fuse if that happens."

"So would I, I think," Aron said.

"Anything new on the relationship front?" Yahatha asked, with a curious look that Aron couldn't quite make out.

"Who could I have met?" Aron asked incredulously.

"Penny... Hana—" Yahatha hinted.

"Penny, no. I'll tell you more about her in a minute. Hana—"

"Ah?" Yahatha drew out a wry smile.

"It's not like that. I... I'll tell you about that later, too. Not today."

"Fine. Well, I have some big news," Yahatha said. Then he looked straight at Aron with a serious face. "But first, you have to promise not to laugh."

"Ok," Aron replied, suspicious.

"I'm engaged," Yahatha said.

"What? That's great news! Why would I laugh about that?" Aron asked.

Yahatha held up a finger, then said. "Her name is Joy."

Aron struggled but failed to stifle a chuckle. "Seriously?"

"Yes," Yahatha said with a resigned sigh.

"Hey, Hana!" Aron called.

"Yeah?" She responded, turning to come back.

"Hahaha is engaged!"

"Wow! Really? That's so fain!" Hana gushed.

"To a girl called Joy," Aron said with a smile.

Hana couldn't help herself; she let out a loud laugh.

"I'm so sorry," she said. "Are you serious, though?"

"Yeah," Yahatha said.

"Well, that's good news! I'm happy for you," Hana said, still struggling to suppress her smile. She gave Aron a knowing look.

"It's not that funny," Yahatha said.

"It is!" Hana snorted.

"You know, you guys are pretty childish."

"Yeah, we are, but so are you," Aron retorted.

"Fine. But you can't laugh about it when you meet Joy. Fain?"

"I would never!" Hana responded. "I can laugh with you, but not in the face of someone I don't know."

"Thank you," he said. Then he turned to Penny. "Did you see anything you like?"

"Hold up, you're not going to tell us about Joy? When can we meet her?" Hana asked.

"Oh, no, we'll talk. I just thought we should order first," Yahatha said.

"Ok, fine."

Yahatha put together their order using the device embedded in the table. Then they all sat back to wait.

"So, come one! Tell us about Joy," Hana said.

"Uh. She's human. She comes from Weal, so she is a big-city girl. She's not as tall as I am," Yahatha said.

"That all could be describing anyone!" Hana exclaimed.

"It doesn't describe you," Aron pointed out.

"What, I'm not human?" Hana asked.

"I wouldn't be surprised," Yahatha smiled.

Hana laughed. "Ok, but where did you meet her?"

"She joined our crew about six months ago in a customer-facing role."

"Come one, give us more!" Hana said.

"Hana, you're not even giving him a chance to talk!" Aron laughed.

"I don't know what else to say, anyway," Yahatha said.

"Well, is she quiet or loud?" Hana asked.

"She's a talker. Not quite as nosey as you are, though," Yahatha said.

"Fine. I won't ask any more questions," Hana said, throwing her hands in the air.

Yahatha turned to Aron and started to ask, "How long do you think this will —"

"Yeah, you got me," Hana laughed. "So, short hair or long hair? And what colour is it?"

Yahatha rolled his eyes at Aron, who just shrugged in reply.

"Short, usually brown hair," Yahatha said.

"Usually brown?" Aron asked.

"It was bright pink when I met her. She has what she calls 'whimsical weeks' where she dyes her hair some colour, then changes it back," Yahatha explained.

"What does she do?" Hana asked.

"I told you, she's a CSR on our ship."

"That's customer service representative," Aron translated for Penny's sake.

"Ok, this is the important one. When can we meet this 'Joy'?" Hana asked. She gave Yahatha an unnecessarily dramatic "serious" look.

"Well, as I told Aron, our ship will be around for a week."

"How long are we here for?" Hana asked Aron.

"Hana, do you ever check the schedule?" Aron asked.

"Not really. Although I did this time and just forgot."

"We'll be here a week," Aron said.

"Ok, great! We'll have plenty of time to catch up then," Hana said, happy.

"Yeah, we have plenty of time. I would have brought Joy to meet you this morning, but she already had plans to meet her own friends."

"Also, Hana, I'll be putting the ship out into cold storage," Aron added.

"Oh, rats!" Hana whined. "That means I have to go back and stay with my dad!"

"Yeah, well, you're welcome to go down and stay with my parents if you like," Yahatha said. "I mean, my room will remain free."

"You live on the surface too?" Penny asked.

"My parents do. My family is rich," Yahatha said.

"Just what I was saying!" Hana told Penny. Hana turned and gave Aron a victorious smile.

"Ok, I don't know the backstory of that," Yahatha said. "But my parents are actually rich. As in, writing an open letter to the dean about how scholarships are bad for everyone, giving poor people false hope and subjecting the kids of people of substance to bad influences."

"That was your parents?" Aron asked.

"Yeah, didn't I tell you?" Yahatha laughed.

"Nope. They must be thrilled about the new inclusive school."

"Thrilled? I wouldn't be surprised if they helped make it happen!"

"Wait, what happened?" Hana asked.

"I got a scholarship to the high-school Yahatha attended the first year they offered scholarships. One of the parents wrote a letter to convince the school to shut the whole scholarship program down," Aron explained.

"I thought Hana said you two met in college?" Penny asked.

"We did. Technically we were at the school at the same time. But we didn't meet until college," Aron said. "It was a big school, and Hahaha was the year above me."

"And what's wrong with an inclusive school? Isn't that good?" Penny asked.

"An 'inclusive' school is a way to get around the non-selective laws. Basically, the government said schools weren't allowed to accept only rich people, and a few scholarships per year were no longer good enough. So then schools like ours built 'inclusive schools' – separate campuses for poorer students. They claim it's one school, but there's no interaction between them."

"I haven't ever heard any of this stuff." Hana sulked.

"Eh. I tell Aron that stuff because he's met my parents. But it's not something you just talk about," Yahatha sighed. "You must know how it is with family issues, Hana."

"Not really. Hana tells everyone everything," Aron said.

"I do," Hana said.

"Well, I hope you don't take it as a personal slight if I have trouble being as open with things," Yahatha said.

"When you put it like that—" Hana sighed.

"Thank you. But I think you must know most of it anyway."

"Do you still talk to your parents? Or have you cut them off completely now?" Aron asked.

"I never talk to them now. Not worth the aggravation. It's easy when I spend all my time out in deep space."

"Will you invite them to the wedding?"

"Are you kidding? They'd never approve of Joy. She's *poor* – supposedly, that's a moral failing on her part. I'll probably introduce her to them, just so she knows why we'll never see them again after that," Yahatha laughed. "Enow about me!"

They were notified by a buzz that their food was ready to collect. Hana drew the short straw and left to get the food from the kitchen window.

"So, Penny, how do you come into things?"

Penny wasn't sure how to respond, so she looked to Aron.

"Ah, that's something I was hoping to talk to you about," Aron said.

Yahatha had a curious look on his face. "Go on."

Aron lent in closer to Yahatha and whispered. "Penny was part of a payment made to me for goods I delivered to Tungol."

Yahatha's face turned to puzzled disbelief. "Seriously?"

"That's why I wanted to talk to you. Do you know Tun?" Aron asked.

"A very little," Yahatha replied, still looking concerned.

"I can't read the device's interface. I don't know how to set her free. I was hoping you knew how to read it. Or knew someone who would," Aron explained.

"Oh! Thank goodness!" Yahatha said with relief.

"What?" Aron asked, confused.

"I thought you were intending to keep her a slave!" Yahatha explained.

"No way! I could never do that!" Aron protested.

"Hence why I was so bemused! Well, I'll be happy to try and help you! Let me take a look," Yahatha said, holding his hand out for the device.

"Are you sure? I don't want to involve you in something that will get you in trouble."

"Don't worry about that. Just give me the thing," Yahatha said, waving dismissively. Then he held out his hand again.

Aron pulled the slave-bolt out of his bag, entered the code, and handed it to Yahatha.

"Gralu! Sem pers Tun?" Yahatha asked Penny, taking the device and poking around at it.

"Musin! Kra pers Tun," Penny replied.

"Sem hast gat Tun?"

"Gat."

"You have a very proper pronunciation. Not that I'm one to judge. My Tun has a distinct regional dialect, I'm told," Yahatha said. "But what does 'Musin' mean?"

"It means 'hello', doesn't it?" Penny said, confused.

"I don't know. I've never heard that word before. You're probably right; I don't know a lot of Tun. Remind me to look it up when I'm done with this."

"What did you two actually say?" Aron asked.

"He asked if I spoke Tun first, then asked if I don't read it," Penny said.

Yahatha kept poking around at the device.

Finally, he set it down and announced. "Well, I have bad news and good news."

"Bad news first," Aron said.

"The bad news is that this language isn't Tun. It's Leat. At least, I believe it is based on the little I know of Leat," Yahatha explained.

"Maggots," Aron exclaimed.

"The good news is that I know enough Leat to find the language options. I just managed to switch it to English."

"Fain!" Aron said. "But I guess the buttons are stuck in Leat."

"That's not Leat. I don't know what language that is," Yahatha said. "Oh. More news (I'm not sure whether it is good or bad) is that the device is saying 'device error; no implant connexion.'"

"What?" Aron asked.

"I think this thing is a dud. It doesn't appear to work. I mean, you can put the code in to unlock it, but that's it. I don't know if it does anything."

"You mean, belike I'm already free of it?" Penny asked.

"Belike? I'm just the language guy. I don't know how these things work," Yahatha replied.

Aron didn't look convinced. "What about the time you fainted when we were on that walk?"

"Ah. You're right," Penny said, looking crestfallen.

"It could just be a coincidence," Aron added.

Hana returned with the tray of food. "What's going on?"

"The device claims it doesn't work. But we don't know if it actually doesn't work, or if it is erroneously claiming it doesn't work."

"Ah. That's tricky," Hana said.

"At least it's in English now," Aron said.

"Nevermind," Penny said. "Thank you all for trying to help me."

"We'll figure this out, Penny. I mean, we're slowly getting there," Aron promised.

"Oh! Hahaha, can you look up 'musin'?" Penny asked.

"Oh right," Yahatha said. He pulled out his phone and found his English to Tun dictionary. "Ah. You might want to stop greeting people that way."

"What does it mean?"

"It means 'slave'."

Aron slapped the table. "This explains how all those people knew you were a slave. You were literally introducing yourself that way."

"Hold on, that doesn't seem right. 'Slave' is 'prar', isn't it?" Penny asked, confused.

"No, that means 'dirt'," Yahatha said. But then he suddenly doubted himself and looked the word up.

"Are you sure? I thought that was 'nin'."

"Well, 'nin' also means dirt. Or, more specifically, soil. See for yourself," Yahatha showed Penny the relevant definitions.

Penny looked really confused. "Nobody has ever referred to me as a slave using 'musin'. Petror explicitly taught me to use it to greet people. When they're talking about slaves, it's always been 'prar'. If you want to buy a slave, you go to the 'prar-flust'," she said.

"Well, look at this: 'prarfek' – crop. It literally means dirt growth."

"Or grown by slaves. It is traditionally a slave-dominated workforce," Penny pointed out.

"I'm only telling you what the dictionary says."

"I know. It's just … unexpected."

"Nevermind, let's put it out of our minds and celebrate the engagement of Joy and Hahaha!" Aron said.

"Oh, man! That sounds so ridiculous!" Yahatha laughed.

"I'm sure it will be a marriage full of mirth!" Hana smiled.

"We should raise a toast to the happy couple!" Penny added.

"Nicely done, Penny!" Aron laughed.

"Penny, I do believe we're going to be good friends," Yahatha said.

Penny smiled.

— — — — —

Yahatha needed to return to work after the meal, but they arranged to meet again another day. Before taking Penny back to the ship, Aron and Hana decided to take Penny on a tour of the sights of the Angish Spaceport.

The first sight they took her to see was the Great Glass Floor, an open plaza between the creeper stations, which had, as the name suggested, a transparent floor. (Aron pointed out that it technically was not actually made out of glass but a transparent ceramic.) The vast expanse of the clear floor allowed people to look down upon the islands of Angish below. Even at this time of the morning, there were many people there.

Despite this being Hana's idea, she didn't dare to step out onto the transparent floor, instead staying on the terraced seating surrounding it. Aron took Penny out to the centre. There they stood, looking down at the islands of Angish below, which were just starting to receive the first light of morning. Aron pointed out various locations on the islands to Penny. In particular, he pointed out the approximate location of Morton Creek on the large island directly below the spaceport.

Afterwards, they headed to the amphitheatre, where a local amateur theatrical group was just beginning a free performance. Although Hana and Aron agreed that the troupe's performance was more skillfully executed than many previous groups' performances. But they soon found the substance of the play not to their taste. So they decided to move on.

Their next stop was the main retail street. This was a wide street lined with high-end shops with fancy facades. Their first stop was for over-priced ice cream before heading down the lines of shops. Hana took Penny into a clothing store, and this time it was Aron's turn to hang back at the edge where he felt more comfortable.

Then they headed into a large department store, browsing each of its departments.

"There's so much in here!" Penny exclaimed.

"Yeah, it's a bit different to the places we've been shopping elsewhere."

"What about Beadful?" Aron asked.

"We only went to the clothing stores, remember?"

"Oh yeah."

"What do people do with all this stuff?"

"Well, in this particular section, we just look at the things without looking at the price tags," Hana said, gesturing to the high-priced wares around them.

"Why don't we look at the price tags?"

"So you can keep the fantasy that you're not buying it because you don't need it. Take this coffee machine. It's a nice coffee machine, but I'm choosing not to buy it because I don't need it. If I look at the price tag, I now have a second reason I wouldn't buy it. Because it's... what? Two thousand credits for this? I wouldn't pay **that** much for this even if I could afford it!" Hana said.

"Yeah, Hana thinks she invented 'fantasy shopping'," Aron said with a roll of his eyes.

"I did," she replied.

"You invented a new name for what everyone else calls window shopping."

"Window shopping could be looking at anything! Fantasy shopping has a purpose!"

Finally, they stopped at the nearest food court for their next meal. They were in the middle of eating their food when the food court's giant pocket-watch sculpture commenced its 9am chiming. This involved the hands spinning, coloured lights flashing, and several flaps opening and closing to allow animatronic mice to run in and out at various places. Penny found this delightful and didn't even notice Hana's sigh of annoyance.

— — — — —

When they returned to the ship, they found Marc wide awake and staring at a screen.

"You guys were gone a long time. How was Hahaha?" Marc asked.

"Hahaha is good. We did a little sightseeing after he went back to work," Aron replied.

"What did you see?"

"The Glass Floor, the shops, that big pocket watch thing," Penny said.

"Oh, that thing is annoying!" Marc exclaimed.

"What's wrong with it?" Penny asked, shocked.

"Every hour, it plays the exact same song at a ridiculous volume!" Hana said a bit louder than she intended.

"Precisely," Marc said.

"Well, I liked it," Penny said defiantly.

"Good for you, Penny. Don't let Hana, Marc, or even the thousandth playing of that tedious, repetitive song change your mind!"

Hana laughed.

"Did Hahaha figure out your thing?" Marc asked.

"He switched the language. We don't know if it's working," Penny said.

"What?"

"She might already be free of it. Alternatively, we might never be able to free her," Hana said.

"Well, that's maggoty," Marc said. "But I think I might have something to cheer you up."

"Oh?" Penny asked.

All ears were on Marc now, and he revelled in the attention for a moment.

"I think I found Penny's parents!"

"What?" Penny gasped.

"Well, I mean, I found their names from an old news broadcast. I'm still trying to find contact details."

"Marc, I don't think I've ever said this before, but you're a genius," Hana said.

"Thank you. I had to hunt for it; most articles only named the kidnapped victims or just how many. And if they did talk about relatives, they wouldn't give a name, just say 'relative of one of the victims'. But I found one little article from a small local newspaper talking to some local residents, whose 5-year-old daughter was kidnapped along with her godparents."

Marc took a deep breath in and stared directly into Penny's eyes.

"Penny – or I should say, Rebecca – would you like to see a picture of your parents?"

"Yes," Penny said in a breaking voice.

Marc turned back to the screen and navigated back to the news article.

"This is your parents, Penny. Martin and Margaret of Swanbrook, on Feng."

The photo was a professionally taken newspaper photo. It showed Martin and Margaret standing together in front of a wooded area, with Margaret crying and Martin with tired eyes and one arm holding his wife.

Marc turned around, expecting to see Penny smiling. Instead, her face looked more distraught.

"They look so scared! So worried!" Penny cried.

"Of course they were!" Hana sympathised. "Don't worry. We're going to find them."

Hana ushered Penny out to allow her to collect herself.

"Well done, Marc," Aron said.

"What? I wasn't trying to make her cry."

"No, I really meant it. Well done finding her parents. Really!"

"Oh. Well, you know, I was just waking up, and the idea of looking for news of the flight Penny was on just hit me."

"Feng... that is so close."

"Well, that's where they were. Who knows where they are now."

"At least we have their names."

"First names only, I'm afraid."

"Still better than nothing. Feng is a tiny place, with only small villages. If they're still there, we'll find them easily. And if they've moved on, maybe someone knows where they've gone."

"That could mean a lot of time stopped at Feng."

"Feng's a decent place to get some cargo, though. Lumber, wooden furniture, any wood products, really. We can afford to make a few trips there."

Aron turned towards the bedroom and then stopped.

"What is it?" Marc asked.

"I was going to turn in, but that's where Hana took Penny."

"Oh," Marc stuttered. "Well, just go; I don't think they'd mind."

Aron opened the bedroom door to find nobody there.

"They must have gone through to the cargo hold," Marc said.

"I think I'll check on Penny first, anyway."

"I'm going to resume my search," Marc said.

Penny returned to the gally a few minutes later, with Hana not far behind.

"I'm sorry, Marc," Penny said.

"Sorry, for what?" Marc asked, his voice full of surprise.

"You did something so nice for me, and all I did was cry."

"And fair enow, too, given the circumstances."

"But I never said thank you."

Marc suddenly felt very self-conscious. "Well, I didn't do it for the thanks."

Penny kissed him on the cheek. "Thank you!"

"You're very welcome."

They exchanged a brief smile before Penny turned to Hana.

"I'm going to turn in now."

"So early?"

"It's been a long day."

"Sure."

You're late, Ciny!
Sorry Cap.
Unload quick. The choppers will be here for the ship, soon.
I found three rings, seven earrings, two necklaces, and a nice watch.
Grub's up, grubs!
Well done, Penny. Very good finds.
Put all your weight on her shoulders. Straps won't hold well enow if she wakes up.

Water!
No!
Penny! Come! Help me dump the failed one.
You're learning things quickly, Penny.

Episode VII. Pew pew pew!

"I hate being home. My family are unbearable!" Hana groaned over the phone.

"You hate being home; you complain about not coming home enow," Aron said, pacing around the garden of his parent's house in the dark.

"We don't come home enow!" Hana insisted. "That doesn't mean I want to spend months here each time."

"It's only been a week," Aron pointed out. "And barely that."

"It feels like a month. When are you coming back to the port?"

"Tomorrow, actually. Marc is planning on meeting someone, and I'm going to try to get some paperwork done."

"Who is Marc going to see?" Hana asked quickly.

"I don't know!" Aron shrugged. "All he told me is that I don't know whomever it is. How's Penny doing?"

"Relax, I'm taking care of her," Hana said. "I'm making a garlic-yogurt-baked chicken for dinner tonight."

"That sounds really good!" Aron said.

"Hopefully. I'm getting Penny to help when she's free. We'll see how it goes."

"Where is she?" Aron asked.

"Taking a shower, not that it's any of your business," Hana snorted. "Still don't know why you won't tell your parents about her!"

"They freak out about us flying in space enow as it is! What am I going to say? 'Hey mum, you know how you never want us going into space? Well, we were paid a slave on one trip, and now we are trying to keep it secret from the police!'"

"Yeah, well, Penny witnessed one of my uncle and aunt's little spats this morning. It wasn't pleasant," Hana said, rolling her eyes.

"I thought you said you were taking care of her!" Aron laughed.

"I **am** taking care of her!" Hana cried.

"Sorry, shouldn't be making jokes! What was it this time?"

"Nothing, as usual," Hana made another snorting sound. "My uncle ate the good eggs instead of the cheap ones my aunt bought for him. She's not speaking to him now. At least that means it's quiet."

"What? Why does she even care about eggs?" Aron asked in disbelief.

"I don't even know!" Hana sighed. "They're not even good; they're just a more expensive brand! She just hates him. But she can't leave or kick him out, or she'd have to get a job."

"Well, why doesn't he leave? Or why don't he and your dad kick her out?" Aron asked.

"Everything is in her name. They'd have to take her to court or something. Nobody has the time or money for that."

Aron sighed. "At least your dad is sane."

"Oh, no; he's totally barmy," she laughed. "But he's a nice barmy."

Aron decided not to engage with that comment. "Well, I aim to be at the ship around midday tomorrow. If you want, you can come and join me."

"Ah. I'm not sure I can. I need to help my dad with some stuff. I could drop Penny off there and come back later in the afternoon, though."

"Oh. Well, ok, I guess," Aron said. "Get your stuff done quickly."

"As quick as I am able!" She said with a cheery voice. "I'll see you later!"

"Bye," he hung up the phone. Then he stopped, turned and looked for a moment up at the lights of the spaceport almost directly above. Finally, with a sigh, he headed inside for dinner.

— — — — —

Hana and Penny arrived at the ship at precisely 12 o'clock. They were surprised to be greeted by Yahatha instead of either Aron or Marc.

"Ah, Penny, Hana, you're here! Hello! Welcome!" Yahatha said, greeting them with a huge smile.

"Where is Aron? And Marc?" Hana asked.

"Hello to you too," Yahatha said, his smile disappearing.

"Hello, Hahaha," Penny said.

"Hello!" Yahatha responded, suddenly chipper again.

"Ok, are we done with the hellos?" Hana asked.

"We will be as soon as you have said it," Yahatha teased.

"Hello," Hana said impatiently.

"To answer your earlier question, Aron is up in the cockpit, under the console," Yahatha said, pointing.

"Hello!" Aron's voice called back.

"Now, now, Aron. We're done with the hellos. Hana doesn't like them," Yahatha laughed. "Marc is in the cargo hold. He's... well, I don't know what he's doing."

"Do you and Marc not get along or something?" Penny asked. "I don't think I've ever seen you two together."

"We get along fine. I only arrived a minute ago. I don't have the history with Marc that I do with Aron or Hana, though," Yahatha explained. "I hope he doesn't feel excluded, though."

"Nah. Marc excludes himself more than anything. I think he sees you just as Aron's friend," Hana said.

"I should put in more effort," Yahatha said, thinking. Hana wasn't quite sure he'd heard her.

"What are you doing here?" She asked.

"You are full of questions today!" Yahatha said, snapping out of his self-absorption.

"It's been a fair set of questions, given the circumstances," Hana reasoned.

"Sure. I'm waiting here for Joy," Yahatha explained, and then he glared at Hana with a playful smile.

Hana rolled her eyes. "Why here?" She asked.

"I knew you'd ask that. I could have just told you, but you seem to like playing the question game."

Hana just rolled her eyes again, this time for Penny's benefit. "Sometimes he's like this."

"She's coming back from the surface. And given that your ship is on the way from the creepers to my ship, I thought I'd meet her here and introduce her to you while I was at it," he said.

"Ok, next question," Hana said. "Why are you holding that wrench."

"Because I asked him for it just before you came in," Aron said, suddenly appearing behind Yahatha and surprising him.

"Sorry, Aron," Yahatha said apologetically, handing over the wrench.

"No worries," Aron said.

At this point, Joy arrived behind Hana and Penny and said, "Hello."

Hana hadn't heard her come in and jumped. "Gave me a fright!" She said.

"Hello, Possum," Yahatha said, blowing a kiss. "Sorry about Hana; she's forgotten how greetings work today."

"Hello, Hana," Joy said.

"Hello, I'm Hana," Hana said. "But you know that."

"Yes, I got that," Joy said.

"I think she likes introducing herself," Aron said.

"Yeah, she did the same to me," Penny said. "Hi, I'm Penny."

"And I'm Aron. Welcome to my ship."

"Thank you. Nice to meet you at last," Joy said, giving him a small wave.

"Yeah, you too. I'll go get Marc," Aron said.

"No, I'll go," Yahatha said. "Making an effort," he whispered to Penny.

There was an awkward pause for a moment where nobody knew what to say.

"I've heard so much about you all," Joy said.

"Well, we've been dying to meet you. Yahatha isn't very good at talking about people," Hana said. "Well, not *seriously* talking about people."

"No, he's not," Joy laughed.

"So tell us a bit about yourself."

"Oh." Joy was a little thrown by this. "Well, I come from Weal, the Rostha district. It's all big industries there. I figured a space-based job would be cleaner."

"Hah!" Hana snorted.

"What about you?"

"I grew up on the spaceport here on the spaceport," Hana said.

"What do you do for fun growing up on a spaceport? I'm not sure I'd have liked that." Joy responded.

Hana looked a bit indignant. "You can do anything you can do on the surface. More in the case of Angish."

"Oh."

Yahatha returned with Marc and introduced them, oblivious to the awkwardness.

"Hana, Hahaha says you like cooking," Joy said.

"I love cooking! Ask Penny; I've force-fed her a lot this week!"

"I can't say I needed to be forced to eat," Penny laughed.

"I started a public food journal. Perhaps you could write a guest post sometime," Joy said.

"What do you write about?" Hana asked.

"Just recipes I've tried, things I'm experimenting with, that sort of thing."

"Oh! Show me!" Hana said, dragging Joy away. Penny followed, and Marc disappeared into the hold again.

Yahatha pulled Aron aside.

"So?" He asked expectantly.

"She's friendly. She shares your love of cooking. I can see why you like her," Aron said.

"Well, I can't see how I could not like her," Yahatha said. Then he added with a sneer, "Of course, Tashiya has already said she's too poor and not pretty enough."

"Didn't you say your sister was better than your parents?" Aron asked.

"It's a low bar," Yahatha sighed. "My sister still somewhat believes that money improves people, I think. But she treats people fine. She acts like the people she knows are the exceptions to the rule."

"What are you going to do after you are married?" Aron asked. "Are there private rooms on your ship?"

"There are no private rooms. Well, except for the ship's top officers. There are small shared rooms with open bunks for everyone else," Yahatha said.

"Ah! That could make things awkward," Aron said.

"'Unworkable' is the word we've been using," Yahatha stated. "It's hard enough to find a job on a ship that has private sleeping arrangements. Belike getting two jobs on a ship like that would be near impossible. At least, it is for people at our level."

"So, what will you do?" Aron asked. "You could buy a ship."

"Hah! Not without using my parents' money. And there is no way I'd let them hold that against me."

"Fair," Aron replied.

"We'll try and get some static jobs, at least at the start. That will probably be easier for Joy; not too many static piloting jobs around," Yahatha said.

"I wouldn't expect so."

Yahatha let out a large breath. "But I'll find something. Doesn't have to be something great, so long as it pays the bills."

"Fair enow."

"So, what about you and Hana?" Yahatha whispered.

Aron turned away from the others and whispered his reply. "It's complicated."

"Is it?" Yahatha asked with evident disbelief.

"Well, you were right; I think she is interested in me."

"I told you!" Yahatha said with a forceful whisper.

"And I still can't shake the belief she deserves better," Aron said.

"No way! You think there's someone better than you, do you? I bet she's looked and disagrees."

Aron didn't have a response. He threw his hands up. "You know how I am," He said.

"Yeah. And I wish you could snap out of it," Yahatha said. Then he shrugged. "I know, I know; easier said than done."

Yahahta put his hands on Aron's shoulders and stared straight into Aron's eyes to drive home his point. "You can do this."

"I know," Aron said, breaking the eye contact.

"Good," Yahatha replied, patting him on the back. "Ignore that voice in your head and just tell her how you feel."

"I will," Aron promised, unsure if he was telling the truth.

"Hahaha, I think we should be going," Joy called.

Yahatha quickly checked his watch.

"Oh, yes! We have to run," Yahatha said. "I'll call back in later the afternoon. Perhaps we can go somewhere for dinner."

"Ok!" Aron replied.

"Nice meeting you all," Joy waved. The sentiment was returned three-fold.

Hana headed towards the door also. "I'll see you later," she said to Aron.

"Where are you going?" Yahatha asked.

"I need to go help my dad," Hana replied.

And with that, the three left.

"Are they gone?" Marc asked, appearing again.

"Yes. Were you hiding?" Penny asked.

"No! Honest! I was just organising the stuff I have in the hold," Marc replied. "I didn't realise they'd be gone so quick."

"Well, we're going to dinner with Hahaha, if you'll be back for that," Aron said.

"Yeah, I can do that," Marc replied. Then he turned to Penny, "So, how was your time with Hana's family?"

"It was ... an experience," Penny said.

"A nice safe answer," Marc laughed.

"Do you know them?" Penny asked.

"Only from Hana's stories," Marc laughed.

"Hahaha and I were there studying the night before an exam once," Aron said. "Definitely an experience."

— — — — —

Later in the afternoon, spaceport time, Yahatha returned to the ship for one last visit, as promised. His cruiser was due to leave the next day. Hana was still out with her father. Penny and Marc had been helping Aron with the bookwork until Marc got a call.

Penny and Aron were glad for an excuse to take a break and a chance to stretch their legs. So Yahatha, Aron, and Penny decided to take a stroll through the docking quadrant. They left the ship and headed in the direction of the nearest plaza.

The walk took them past other docking bays, with people managing the moving stacks of crates and containers into and out of their vessels. This was done mainly by automated systems. But there were a few small ships with people moving the cargo manually.

"What kind of name is Yahafa?" Penny asked.

"Hah! Firstly, it's Yahatha."

"Oh! Sorry!"

"Don't worry about it. I get it all the time. I don't really know where the name comes from! I think it comes from Kanang. Belike, anyway. Both of my parents had mixed heritage. Yahatha comes from my mum's side, and they're mostly from Kanang," Yahatha replied. "But don't call me Yahatha."

"You don't like it?" Penny asked, surprised.

"I like it fine. But my friends don't use it. It's only work and other official things where I'm called Yahatha. So now it sounds very formal," Yahatha explained.

"Withal, nobody has trouble pronouncing 'Hahaha'," Aron added.

"What about you? Are you going to go by Penny or Rebecca?" Yahatha asked.

"I still don't know yet. Rebecca is my real name. But I've been Penny for so long, that feels more like my name." Penny said.

"You could compromise and go with Becky," Yahatha suggested with a shrug.

"How is that a compromise?" Aron laughed.

"It's halfway between, right? Rebecca, Becky, Penny."

"Not your best." Aron shook his head.

"It's fain."

"Penny, Rebecca, they're both good names. We'll call you whatever you want," Aron said, turning to Penny.

But Penny had stopped a few steps back. She was watching a man across the way, who had his back to them, loading crates on a cart to be moved.

"What are you looking at?" Aron asked.

"I think that's Jor," Penny said quietly.

"Is it someone you know?" Yahatha asked.

"How can you tell?" Aron looked a little concerned.

"He was watching us as we walked up. But as we got close, he saw me looking at him, and he turned away. But I'd swear it was him."

"Jor!" Yahatha yelled. "No response. Jor!"

The man turned and signed 'quiet' at them. He looked furtively around before walking over.

"Ah... Perhaps you shouldn't have done that!" Aron suggested.

"Why not?" Yahatha asked.

But there was no time for a response; the man was now close. He stopped a few paces away from them.

"Don't go yelling that name!" The man said gruffly.

"It is you!" Penny gasped.

"Yes, it's me," he growled. "But don't go yelling that name. It's not safe here; I'm trying to be legitimate. Here, I'm known as Mike."

"Do you recognise me?" Penny asked.

"Of course, silly girl," Jor said.

"It's good to see you!"

"Yeah, I'm glad to see you alright. Err... Captain was quite mad when Noggs shipped you out. Taught him a severe lesson; I can't figure out why Noggs didn't see that coming. But the Captain was hoping you'd be in the penny-come-quick, of course."

"I might have done," Penny said, with a careful glance over at Aron.

"Course you would. Not that you could now. I'm legitimate, as I mentioned. We got a full load of the crew here. Getting some zeds and jives. And to pick up some pigeon cargo brought from Tungol."

"Penny's part of our 'crew' now," Aron interjected.

"Yeah? And who are you?" Jor asked, raising himself up.

"I'm Aron. And this is Yahatha." Aron's voice faltered as Jor gave him a withering stare.

Jor sized Aron up for a moment.

"Alright." He sniffed dismissively. Then he turned to Penny. "Anyway, good to see you, girl. And if you want, find the keys on Hiver, near or far. Just remember: Jack's comforted a wren. And maybe I'll see you around sometime."

Without another word, Jor turned away from them. Yahatha looked at Penny to see if any of that meant anything to her. But her face told him she was as confused as he was. They turned to Aron, but he had something else on his mind.

"Wait!" Aron yelled after Jor.

Jor stopped, turned, and stomped back towards them with a glower.

"What do you want?" He growled impatiently.

"How do we disable Penny's slave bolt?" Aron asked.

The glower immediately disappeared.

"Hah! Ain't that the best joke!" Jor addressed Penny directly. "You ain't got one, Penny! Not as I'm aware, leastways; lest you got it after you left us."

"You were always threatening me with it," Penny said.

Jor let out another sudden (but quiet) laugh. "That one: Ciny changed its language, and we couldn't change it back! We used it to keep you and Bill in line when you were little brats! But I can check if you want. Do you have it?"

Aron pulled it out of his jacket pocket and reluctantly handed it to Jor. Jor took it, looking each way down the street.

"Ah. You managed to change the language, I see." He poked it twice, then looked right into Penny's eyes. "Feel anything?"

"No."

"No agonising, debilitating pain?"

"No."

"There, proof. I've switched this thing off. If you had one, your implant should be trying to prevent your escape. If you want more proof, you can look here, above the eighth vertebrae. Well, of course, you can't. Your mates can look." Jor pulled her head forward and then yanked her collar down a bit. "No scar. The surgery is good. We make it heal up nice, and it's always hard to see. But that scar is always there. Now look." Jor pulled his own collar down. Sure enough, between his shoulder blades was the faintest of scars.

"You were a slave?" Penny asked.

"Was. Stopped being a slave a long time afore I knew you," Jor said, quietly sliding the slave bolt into his back pocket while they were distracted by this revelation.

"But you were a slaver," Penny said, a look of incomprehension on her face.

"When the choice is to do it or be it, it's pretty simple. You understand that, right? But the Captain was a good man. Gave me my freedom with none of the conditions that others might have. Now, off you go, little girl. I have work and don't need nor want it entangling you now."

He walked back across the way to his crates. Penny watched him the entire time. Aron and Yahatha watched them both, unsure of how to proceed.

Jor loaded the last of the boxes quickly. Then with a severe glance, he disappeared through a nearby door.

"Penny?" Aron said quietly.

"Yes?"

"You're properly free now!"

"I am!" Penny smiled. "But we need to move. Chances are law enforcement is on its way."

She turned and led the way back to the ship.

"What? Why?" Aron asked, shocked.

"I don't know what Jor is doing, but it's some crime."

"He said he was legitimate!" Aron protested, confused.

"Exactly. That's part of the cant. It's the same words but a completely different language. So they can discuss their work whilst everything they say sounds innocent. Now, come on! Quickly!"

"Don't need to tell me twice," Yahatha said, running off ahead.

"I didn't mean run!" Penny called after him. But he kept going, so Penny and Aron jogged after him.

—   —   —   —   —

Once they were back at the ship, they bundled themselves inside and closed the door to the threat they knew wasn't following them.

"Penny, you're free! From that thing, I mean. This is so exciting!" Aron gushed.

"I am!" Penny was smiling from ear to ear.

"Technically, she was free all along," Yahatha said.

"Well, sure, that thing didn't make her a slave. And we... well, I hope Penny didn't feel like we were treating her as a slave."

"I didn't," Penny interjected.

"Good. Anyway, my point was that while we thought the slave-bolt might work, it was keeping her as a slave."

"Just to make sure it's clear, I definitely feel like I've been free for a while. You guys treat me like a person, you know?" Penny said, clearly affected by her words.

"Well, good. But treating you as a person isn't doing something special, though," Aron said.

"It's more than anyone else has done for me. Ever since I can remember, I've just been someone to be told what to do to make others' lives easier. Or an inconvenience to be gotten rid of."

"What about Bill and Jor?"

"No, Penny is right, Aron. Maybe those were exceptions; I actually don't know. And it'd be nice if everybody acted as they should, but the three of you actually did something special. Most other 'good people' would have just given up and found an easy way out," Yahatha said.

"Fine. But the main thing is Penny being free."

Aron gave Penny a friendly pat on the shoulder. Penny smiled in return. But pretty quickly, Penny's smile turned to a concerned frown.

"What is it?" Aron asked, concerned.

"Jor took the slave bolt!" She stated.

Aron checked his pockets.

"I guess he did. Does it matter? It's a dud, right? Did he lie about that?"

"No, he didn't lie. I've seen those scars he's talking about; they are always there. I always just assumed I had it too," Penny said, unconsciously rubbing her neck. "But I'm worried about what he wants it for. Perhaps he intends to reuse it."

They paused for a minute to consider this. But Aron was struck with another question.

"Penny, when you said you would have joined the pirates, was that true?"

"Technically, I said no such thing," Penny lied. "I told him I'd join the penny-come-quick. It's just a way to ask if the person is in a safe situation."

Aron looked puzzled for a moment. "Oh, right. The cant."

"How do you know what's straight English and what's not?" Yahatha asked.

"You learn the trigger phrases and the expected responses. It's nothing complicated."

"I thought for a moment that Jor was telling you to go to Hiver to find the keys for your slave bolt. Do you know what that was about, Penny?" Yahatha asked.

"I don't know," Penny said, thinking. "Definitely part of the cant. He forced it in; he should have made the words fit the conversation. But I don't know what it means."

"Marc would... Wait, where is Marc?" Aron asked, only just noticing his absence.

"He was here when we left," Yahatha said. "Maybe he left to see the friends he was talking to on the phone?"

"Those ones are down on the planet. Besides, if Marc left early to see the other friends, he would have left a note saying where he was gone."

"He probably hasn't gone far, then," Yahatha said.

"Probably. But it's not like him."

"He'll show up. Give him fifteen minutes; if he's still not back, call him and see where he got to. In the meantime, we should think of something to do to celebrate Penny's freedom," Yahatha said.

"You're right," Aron said. "Let's find somewhere fancy to go. I think this is worth splurging a bit!"

"What kind of fancy? Tetsuya's or Elements?" Yahatha asked.

Aron grimaced. "Well, I can't afford Tetsuya's."

"Oh, good. Me neither," Yahatha said with a sigh.

"So I guess it's Elements. Unless you know a third, reasonably priced but still fancy restaurant."

"Nope."

"Me neither," Penny added.

"I need to go back to my ship for a bit. I'll need to change to go to Elements; can't go in overalls," Yahatha said. "Let me know when Marc and Hana return."

"Will do."

"See you later, Hahaha," Penny said.

"I'll see you both later," Yahatha said, clicking his fingers as he headed out the door.

Barely a minute later, Hana returned.

"Hello! I'm back," she said. "Where was Hahaha running off to?"

"Back to his ship to get changed. We're celebrating!"

"What for?" Hana asked. Then she got visibly excited. "Did you find Penny's parents?"

"Ah, no. But Penny is completely free," Aron said. "We've confirmed that the slave bolt is a dud."

"Oh, wow! But how?"

Aron wasn't quite sure how to explain it. "Penny? Do you want to tell her?"

Penny was ready for this. "Do you remember I told you about Jor?"

"Uh, the slave guy?" Hana asked, unsure.

"That's right. We met him on the road. That slave bolt was a dud. I never had one installed."

"Oh, great! Oh! I'm so excited!" Hana took Penny by the hands and squeezed them.

"So we're going to going to Elements—"

"Oh!" Penny interrupted. "Oh, maggots! We need to call Marc! Now!"

"What, why?" Aron asked, concerned.

"I was trying to remember the meaning of some of the stuff Jor had said. Then I remembered that Jor said he was here for a pigeon cargo from Tungol."

"Yeah, so?" Aron asked.

"A pigeon is code for an expendable carrier. We came from Tungol! What if Marc is the carrier? He could be in trouble!"

"No! Marc would never do such a thing!" Hana protested. She looked to Aron. "He wouldn't, would he?"

In a split second, Aron went from sharing Hana's confidence to having a mind full of doubts.

"Uh... I'll call him," he said, reaching for his phone.

He tried to call Marc. "No answer. Where could he have gone?"

"The quad's gone," Hana pointed out. "We could use the locator."

"Good idea," Aron said.

"What's the quad?" Penny asked.

"It's a small four-wheeled thing we rarely use. It's for moving cargo on and off the ship and for short journeys outside the ship. But it has a locator device in case it's stolen or something," Hana explained as Aron pulled its interface up on the nearest ship's computer. It hadn't gone far, so they all headed out to try to find him.

Sure enough, they found the quad parked beside the road not far from where they had seen Jor.

"It looks like he could be involved in whatever Jor was doing," Aron said. "Typical!"

"Given that he hasn't done anything like this before, I don't think it's typical at all!" Hana said.

"But he's always getting into some trouble! Do you think they might have taken him somewhere?" Aron asked Penny.

"I doubt it. Slavers wouldn't do anything to someone unless they did something which caused them problems. They wouldn't do anything to risk getting negative attention until they have no choice."

"Ok. Let's think about this," Aron said, thinking. "So how would this have worked, Penny? Where would they want to do this?"

Penny panicked. "I don't know! I never left the base. I only know what I was told or overheard."

"That's ok. Anything you can tell us."

Penny thought about it for what seemed like a very long time.

"They wouldn't have met the pige... Marc at their ship. They would have chosen a neutral place nearby."

"Here?" Hana asked.

"Not here. This street is too big. It would need to be somewhere quiet but with options for a getaway."

"I guess Marc left the quad and walked to the meeting place," Aron said.

"Have you got a map?" Penny asked.

Hana produced a map on her phone. Penny studied it quite intently for a minute or two.

"Their ship's here; Marc left the quad here," Penny stated, pointing at the map. "So I would guess that this is where they're meeting."

"Let's go have a look," Aron said, starting to move.

"No, wait. This is a more likely spot," Penny said, indicating a fourth location.

"Ok, let's go," Aron said.

They proceeded at a jog to the location Penny had specified. It was a small dead-end alley around a corner from where they found the quad and two from where they'd seen Jor. It was dark and, more significantly, appeared empty.

"I guess this is not it," Hana said.

"Help!" Came a small, weak voice.

"Marc!" Hana cried. Aron, Hana, and Penny all ran toward the voice.

"I'm here. You found me!" Marc said with a groan.

Marc was slumped down behind a discarded industrial refrigerator. There was a significant amount of blood on and around him.

"Marc, what happened?" Aron asked as he dropped to his knees beside Marc.

"Pirates," Marc said.

"I'm going to get help," Hana said. She pulled out her phone and headed back to the main road while dialling.

"I thought it would be easy money," Marc said. "Belike pay off the ship. Just stash the goods in the hold. Hand it over when we reach port."

"Take it easy, Marc," Aron pleaded.

"I didn't realise what it was. It was slave bolts, Aron! For slaves! New slaves! I couldn't let them have them. I told them I wouldn't give it to them and refused the money. But they shot me!"

Penny was backpedalling her way towards the opposite wall of the laneway. Tears were coming to her eyes as she shook her head in disbelief.

"Good on you for standing up to them, Marc," Aron said, his voice failing. "But right now, we need to focus on getting you help. Don't worry; Hana has already called for someone to come."

The response time of the spaceport's emergency services was fast. They could already hear the sirens.

"You hear that, Marc? They're already on the way."

"I'm so sorry, Aron!" Marc coughed.

"You just worry about yourself right now," Aron said as the paramedics ran towards them.

— — — — —

"Do you think he'll pull through?" Penny quietly asked when Aron entered the waiting room.

"I don't know," He lied. He sat down gingerly on one of the seats

"I hope so. I really, really hope so," Penny said.

"So do I," Aron said quietly.

Penny wanted to say something else. But when she opened her mouth, nothing came out.

Aron broke the silence instead. "Do you think it could have been Jor?"

Penny looked at him, puzzled.

"He's the only one I saw," Aron explained. "Anytime I think about what might have happened, I just keep seeing him pulling the trigger."

"Not Jor. It wasn't Jor. Don't get me wrong, Jor is a scunner; he did many terrible things. He's never killed anyone, though." Penny sighed. "At least, that was what he always told me. Maybe he lied."

Aron couldn't sit still. He stood up and started pacing.

"What are you going to do now you're free?" He suddenly asked, attempting to think about something else in order to keep control of his emotions.

"I don't know," Penny said quietly. "I used to think I knew what I'd do, but now I have no idea."

"I think the established tradition when a slave goes free is to give you some money to help them start their life. You could go in search of your family. I don't have much mone—"

"Can't I just come along with you?" She asked.

But that brought Aron back to thinking about the problems. He dropped into a nearby chair.

"To be honest, I don't know what I'm going to do now. I can't fly with two pilots. I'm never going to find another one. Even Hana doesn't like the ship."

"Don't say that. Hana likes it well enough. And I'm not going to give up on Marc yet. He'll pull through."

Aron smiled sadly.

"I wish I could just go in there and —" Aron wasn't quite sure what to say, so abstractly waved his hands, "— and Marc would just be all better."

"Yeah," Penny sighed.

Then Aron sobbed.

"I was always so impatient with him. I never listened. Why? He wasn't a bad brother..." Aron bit his lip to try to stop the tears.

Right at this point, Hana and Yahatha arrived. As soon as Hana saw Aron's state, she ran over to comfort him. Penny shifted to a closer seat to give him a reassuring pat on the back. Yahatha stood off at a distance, for the first time at a loss for what to do or say.

And that's how they were when the doctor arrived to give them the bad news.

Hey! Girl! Both Cap and Jor are gone; dealing with that deserter. So do you know what that means?
Time for my revenge!
It's high time we sell this slave! Let's put her with the others!

Unwrapped, now!
That item. The strong one.
*That item. The strong one.
Here. You dress, we go
*So cheap! I'll buy the ... female too!
I gat two, and maybe I gat more!

Episode VIII. Parents and Partings

"I feel so useless," Hana complained.

"You don't have to do anything," Aron reassured her, sitting beside her with his morning coffee.

"I know, but I'm here to support you guys, and you're the ones doing everything for me," Hana said, throwing her hands up.

"Relax!" Aron said softly.

"Are you sure your mother doesn't mind me staying here? I keep offering to cook, and she says 'no' in a weird way," Hana said, checking her surroundings in case Aron's mother was around.

"I said relax!" Aron said. "It's fine! You're fine!"

Hana took a deliberate breath to calm herself. Then she looked out the window to where Penny was sitting in the grass.

"Penny loves your garden. Wouldn't surprise me if she's never seen a house with a garden before. Or mountains."

"Yeah, well, with all your talk about how we owned land, you had her convinced I lived on a farm!" Aron laughed.

"There are paddocks just across the fence. They probably belong to your uncle or something," Hana said.

"No. Those belong to a woman named Ailis," Aron stated.

Hana gave him an expectant look.

"Second-cousin once removed," he reluctantly clarified.

"How many McNamaras are there around here?" She asked.

"Hah! We're the only McNamaras. It's all my mother's side of the family," Aron explained.

Hana just sighed. "Well, it's nice, quiet, and peaceful. There must be only a dozen buildings in the whole town!"

"I counted. It's eighty-four, including the supermarket, post office, farm supply store, and the church."

"Of course, you've counted!" Hana laughed.

Aron just stared out at the garden for a moment.

"When we were kids, Marc always wanted to be out there running about, and I always wanted to be inside reading. When we were teenagers, I was always outside fixing – or breaking – something, and he was always inside watching TV. Funny how that worked out."

Hana gave him a friendly smile. "I miss him too."

After a moment, she decided to change the subject. "Did they ever track down the ship the pirates were on?"

"They identified the ship; based on where we saw Jor. But it disappeared. They haven't seen any trace of it since it left Angish," Aron said.

"I find that hard to believe!" Hana scoffed. "They have ways of tracking ships through Tuanti space."

"Most of which work by the ship broadcasting its own location," Aron pointed out. "Pirates wouldn't want their ship to do that."

"They have DSPS!" Hana exclaimed.

"Yes. That told the police which direction the pirates were going when they left. Then they went out of range."

"It can't just disappear!"

"The systems only cover the shipping lanes. The ship didn't reappear anywhere further along its last known trajectory. It could be anywhere," Aron explained.

"Bah! It's all excuses!" Hana said.

"Maybe. Anyway, us getting worked up isn't going to help any. Let's do something to take our minds off it. We should go get Penny and take a walk to the creek," Aron suggested.

Hana sighed. "Yeah, I think that's a good idea."

— — — — —

Marc's funeral was a small, family affair. It was held at the Morton Creek High Church, an old red-brick building built between large green trees on a large plot of land. The land had been donated by his great-grandfather.

Marc's cousin Eiles, who was the rector of this parish, led the service. Aron admired her strength in doing this; Eiles had been close with Marc and Aron growing up, despite the more than 10-year age gap. She started by talking about Marc's influence on her, particularly his belief that faith should be shown by actions, not sermons and rituals. But she clearly found sharing her personal feelings difficult and soon retreated to the traditional service.

There was one other deviation from the traditions of the High-Chuch. Marc and Aron's father, Daniel, had requested to say a few words during the service. He got up and gave a rambling monologue about Marc's childhood. He attempted to include a few humourous anecdotes, but these received only muted responses. He then talked about how proud he was of who his son had become. He struggled as he spoke about what a generous and giving person his son had been. His voice failed when he talked about how hard it was to have his son taken away from him. But he rallied and said a final farewell to his son.

After that, Eiles said a few words in prayer before leading the congregation in a song.

After the service, Marc's coffin was carried by his mother, father, brother, two aunts, and one uncle. Eiles led them out the doors of the church to the small cemetery behind the church. Eiles said a few final words, the family said their final goodbyes and the coffin was lowered into the ground.

— — — — —

That night, while Penny took a shower, Aron suggested to Hana that they should go out and look at the stars. They just lay on the small patch of grass for a few minutes, quietly observing the twinkling lights above. Finally, Aron found the courage to say what he had called her outside for.

"Hana," he said quietly.

"Yes?"

"You know you mean a lot to me, don't you?" He asked.

Hana stopped. Every muscle was locked in place. She wondered just what kind of revelation this was going to be.

He continued, "I mean, I just said goodbye to one of the most important people in my life today. I don't want to let another one go without telling them what I feel. So you know that, right?"

"Aron, you mean a lot to me too. Would I even be here otherwise?" She asked.

"Well, that's the thing. Part of me keeps expecting you to realise there's something better for you. You shouldn't be flying my dumb little ship," he said.

Hana figured out what he was trying, but failing, to say.

"Well, you're a bigger idiot than I thought," she said. She rolled over and looked directly at him. "That's not just your ship. It's my ship too."

Aron was taken by surprise. "I'm pretty sure I'm the one that paid for it."

"That was just the financial investment. In the other things, I've invested just as much as you. And do you know why I did that?"

"Uh —"

"Shut up; I'm speaking. It's because I love you. And you love me," she said.

Aron paused for a moment. "I do," he finally said, looking her in the eye.

"Of course you do. You just didn't know how to say the words," she said, rolling back onto the ground. "And I didn't say the words either. Until now, I worried it was because you would never be there. Or that there was something wrong with me. But it's not that at all, is it?"

"No, it's not," he said.

"It's just that you're stupid," she looked directly at him as she said this.

Aron wasn't sure what was happening but decided it was best to play along. "Fine. I've been stupid," he admitted.

Hana laughed. "We've both been stupid! But at least we know that now."

Aron finally had a chance to stop and think about what had just been said.

"That conversation didn't go how I expected it to go."

"Yeah. It was a bit weird." Hana said.

"Well, that's fine. That's who we are," Aron said.

Hana thought for a moment. "Do you mind if I tell people we were secretly dating for the last year?"

Aron laughed. "It's not really a lie. Just don't mention that we weren't in on the secret."

— — — — —

Two days later, while Penny and Hana were eating breakfast, Aron came into the room fully dressed.

"You guys better pack; we're headed to Feng. We're going to look for Penny's parents," he said quickly.

Penny was startled by the sudden announcement and almost choked on her food.

"So soon?" Hana asked while Penny recovered. "Don't you want to stay here with your parents a bit longer?"

"No, that's the last thing I want to do," Aron said, shaking his head. "Besides which, my mum wants you out of the house."

"I told you she doesn't like me!" Hana exclaimed.

"No, not you specifically. Both of you. Mum's not a very social person. I think she needs some alone time to help her deal with things," Aron explained. "Besides, if we leave today, we can take Hahaha; his ship got redirected to Feng for more maintenance. Flying with us will save him spending money flying commercial."

"You're taking the ship?" Hana asked. "You don't mind flying it on a dead run?"

"It's not going to be a dead run. I got some cargo; it's being taken up to the spaceport now."

"How did you organise that?" Hana asked, surprised.

"Uncle Anrai has a friend who needs some equipment moved. And he and Aunty Eimile have some things they want to be shipped to my cousin Christine on Feng. Some furnishings for her new place, I believe. It's not much, but enow cover the costs."

"Oh, so there'll be no pay," Hana said, disappointed.

"No pay for me. I have to pay you guys." Aron said. "You know, eventually."

"Uh huh," Hana said, rolling her eyes at Penny.

"We should find some good cargo on Feng, though."

"Penny, you're being very quiet about all this," Hana said. "We're going to find your parents! Aren't you excited?"

"No, I am. It just hasn't sunk in," Penny said.

"Plus, you haven't given her a chance to say anything before," Aron laughed.

"How are we going to find them?" Penny asked.

"Feng is a small place. How hard could it be?" Aron said.

"You know, this is why we need Marc." Hana started. But she found she couldn't finish that thought.

"Yeah, well, get ready to go. We leave at 11."

—   —   —   —   —

It was nearly twelve when Aron, Hana, and Penny finally headed down the road to Corley. The route followed Morton Creek and then the Greenby River down the valley. Eventually, the natural slopes of the valley gave way to artificial ones as the city's buildings covered the hillsides. Ahead of them, through the valley, they could see the base of the long strands of the creepers rising from its artificial island in the sparkling Inner Sea.

They met Yahatha and had lunch at a small restaurant by the stony beach before heading to the creeper. They arrived just in time for the departure warning and had to run to board before the doors closed. The creeper was full due to the lunchtime rush, and they found themselves squashed against the doors.

At the top station, they pushed their way out through the crowds. Once on the streets of the spaceport, they made their way toward the port district itself. Aron's uncle was at the ship, waiting for them. While Aron talked with his uncle, Hana, Penny, and Yahatha went inside.

"Everything is loaded, then?" Aron asked.

"Thanks for doing this. I don't know what we would have done otherwise; we just couldn't afford to send this stuff over at the regular rate."

"Don't worry about it; we were heading that way anyway," Aron said.

"I need to rush. But thanks again."

"I'll see you next time we're home," Aron said with a wave.

Aron headed inside the ship. Aron half expected to see Marc in there.

"I'm setting up in Marc's bunk. Just letting you know," Yahatha said.

"Of course. You better take the first sleeping shift. That way, you'll also get the last sleeping shift and be refreshed for when you rejoin your ship. Hana and I will take the ship out."

"Thanks; I appreciate that," Yahatha said. He turned and headed to the bedroom.

Aron turned to Hana, who had already gone up to the cockpit. "Hana, let's go."

"Already preparing the ship."

"Are you alright, Penny?"

"Fine."

"Then let's go."

— — — — —

Yahatha appeared again eight hours later, carrying a towel and heading for the shower.

"Morning, Captain! Morning Hana and Penny!" He said, in his usual chipper voice.

"Good evening!" Hana replied.

"Good afternoon!" Aron added.

Yahatha disappeared into the shower.

"Was it just me, or was that weird?" Hana asked.

"Normal for us," Aron replied.

"No! I was expecting Marc."

"Me too," Penny added quietly.

"Same here. Well, not this early," Aron joked. Then he felt terrible.

Hana noticed his reaction.

"You did that to yourself," she said with a sympathetic smile.

"I guess this is going to last for a while." He said.

"I should hope so. Marc shouldn't be forgotten so quickly." Hana said.

Penny yawned.

"Alright, I'm going to bed," she said.

"I'll turn in soon, too," Hana said. Then she looked at Aron again. "I'll wait until Hahaha is out; keep you awake."

"Thanks," he replied.

True to her word, Hana waited until she heard the shower door lock being undone. Then with a quick kiss, she headed quickly off to bed.

Yahatha saw her leave in a hurry.

"What was that about?" He asked slyly.

"She's going to bed," Aron replied.

"Ok, seriously, you have to tell—" Yahatha started.

Aron held up his hand to tell him to stop.

"I talked to her," Aron said.

"Well done you!"

"She did the hard parts, really," Aron admitted.

Aron said nothing more, despite Yahatha's glare. "So?"

"We decided we're a couple."

"Finally!" Yahatha said with a sigh.

"You were right."

"Of course I was!" Yahatha laughed.

— — — — —

Twenty-six hours later, everyone was awake ready for the arrival at Feng.

"How long until we dock?" Hana asked Aron, appearing from the bedroom.

"Two minutes ago," Yahatha replied from the co-pilot's seat.

Hana was shocked. "What! Already? Penny, quick!"

"Already? We had to wait for ages to get a berth! Feng spaceport is tiny! I tried to call you. What were you guys doing back there, anyway?"

"Are we nearly there?" Penny asked.

"We missed it!" Hana cried.

Penny looked deflated.

"Nevermind, I can just play back the approach on the screen," Yahatha said.

"Yeah, while you do that, I'm going to see if Christine is here," Aron said.

Aron went down and opened the outside door to see two customs officials standing in the doorway. He started with surprise.

"Sorry, I didn't expect to see anyone there." He said.

The woman ignored this and started her reading her introduction. "Welcome to Feng Spaceport. My name is Ms Fredenhagen, and this is Mr Sim. We have a flag on your spaceship stating that you entered Tuanti space by way of the Hogian Checkpoint at a time when it was closed, bound for Angish. We're here to check your cargo, passenger, and crew manifests are accurate."

The whole time she talked, her companion, Mr Sim, watched her silently with his hands behind his back.

"Well, I'm not sure how you can do that," Aron laughed.

Ms Fredenhagen didn't see the humour. "We just need to inspect the cargo and check the identification documents of the people on board."

"I know. But that's not going to work."

"Why not?" Ms Fredenhagen asked with a concerned look.

"Because we unloaded the cargo at Angish and ... had a crew change there also," Aron said.

"Why?" Ms Fredenhagen asked.

"Why? Because that's where the cargo was destined."

Ms Fredenhagen considered this. "What about the crew change?"

"The previous crew member died."

"I'm sorry to hear that." Ms Fredenhagen said. "I suppose the passenger disembarked there, also."

"Actually, no. She's still on board. This is her destination."

Ms Fredenhagen made a mark on her notes. "Did you check in with the customs office on Angish?" She asked.

"No."

"Why not?"

Aron shrugged. "I didn't know I needed to. It wasn't mentioned by either the checkpoint or the patrol ship that checked us."

"Well, I'm sorry, but I will have to inspect the ship, its cargo, and all the people on board. And anything which deviates from the manifest will have to be noted. Although, we can certainly put any justifications you have in the notes."

Aron couldn't believe it. "Fine. Can you deal with my crew first? One of us has to rush off to join his normal ship."

"I'm afraid it doesn't work that way. We need to check the cargo before anyone can leave. That could take hours for a ship this size." Ms Fredenhagen said, tapping her notes.

"Well, here's some good news: we're light on cargo this run. But I'll let my crew member know he may be detained."

Aron led the two customs officers into the ship. Hana and Yahatha were a little surprised by their entrance.

"Ms Fredenhagen, this is my crew, Hana Haselvale and Yahatha Ada. And these are customs officers Ms Fredenhagen and, uh, Mr Sim."

"Good morning," Ms Fredenhagen said. "And where is your passenger?"

"She's in the bathroom," Hana laughed. Ms Fredenhagen gave her a quizzical look.

"Well, let's start by checking the identification papers for you three."

"Hahaha, you're going to need to call your ship. We are not allowed to leave until they have inspected the hold."

"Oh!" Yahatha frowned. "Alright then,"

While Yahatha called his ship, Aron and Hana started going through the formalities with Ms Fredenhagen.

At about this point, Penny emerged, having concluded her business. Mr Sim, who had to this point been a mute observer, took a sudden and keen interest in her.

"Hello." He said.

"Hi," Penny replied.

"I'm sorry, you look very familiar," Mr Sim said. "Are you from Feng?"

"I am, but I haven't been here for a long time," she replied.

"I'm sorry, where are my manners," Mr Sim said. "I'm Anndra Sim."

"Penny. Or, rather, Rebecca," Penny said.

Mr Sim laughed. "Careful, I'm a customs agent, which is it?"

"Rebecca. I was kidnapped as a child, and the slavers named me Penny."

Mr Sim seemed startled. He took a closer look at Penny, making her a little uncomfortable.

"You are!" He said, in awe. "You're Rebecca Maguire!" Mr Sim seemed to forget to close his mouth after saying this. Now everyone's attention was on him.

"You know?" Penny asked.

"I know your parents! You're the spitting image of your mother. Oh, they were so devastated when your ship disappeared. Nobody knew what happened, of course."

"Anndra, are you sure about this?" Ms Fredenhagen asked him in a stern voice.

"Of course; it's definitely her."

"What proof do you have that she is who she claims?"

"I don't have any identification," Penny said.

"Well, you wouldn't! Don't worry; the police can do a DNA test and get you interim documents. And you could be back home with your parents in an hour!"

Mr Sim started heading toward the door.

"Mr Sim, I still have an inspection to do!"

"Ms Fredenhagen, I am the superior officer here. I know, ordinarily, I'm not meant to intervene, but this isn't an ordinary situation. Your inspection is clearly a four-ten; frankly, I don't know why you're bothering with it! Now, come, all of you. I'll take you to the police station; they can do the DNA test."

Yahatha returned and spoke to Aron. "The good news is my ship is delayed three hours due to a –" He stopped. "Wait, what's going on?"

"Mr Sim here knows Penny's parents. She'll be home in an hour, apparently."

"Oh! Exciting! I might get to see them!"

Mr Sim and Ms Fredenhagen led them to the port's customs office. From there, Mr Sim continued with them to the spaceport's police station.

The police were more sceptical than Mr Sim had been. They wanted statements from everyone, even from Yahatha. Aron was reluctant to tell them that he had legally been Penny's owner, but at the same time, he felt he couldn't lie.

The DNA test itself was quick and confirmed everyone's suspicions. But getting the interim paperwork took longer than an hour. Unfortunately, this, combined with the time taken gathering statements, meant that Yahatha would not have time to make the trip down to the surface. Before he left, Yahatha said his goodbyes and gave Penny his well-wishes for meeting her parents.

"Are you ready to go?" Mr Sim asked. "Your parents are already expecting you."

"They know she's coming?" Hana asked.

"Of course. The police called them while we were giving our statements," Aron explained.

"Are you coming, Mr Sim?" Penny asked.

"Yes. I requested the rest of the day off. My boss was very understanding, given the circumstances. And please, call me Anndra," Mr Sim explained.

"Ok, Anndra," Penny said. "Let's go."

The ride down the creeper was the longest 55 minutes in Penny's life. Despite this creeper having plenty of seating, Penny stood at the windows taking in every detail she could of the planet on which she was born. When she'd seen her fill of the mountains to the west, she'd shift to the east side and take in the large bay they were descending towards.

"Look at Penny. She's so excited!" Hana whispered to Aron.

"Can you blame her? She hasn't seen her parents in over 20 years."

"I'm jealous," Hana said. "I haven't seen my mum for that long, but I wouldn't be like this if you told me we were headed to see her."

"Don't be silly; I think you'd be excited."

Hana gave him a warning glare as she waited for the punch line. But Aron was deliberately looking the other way.

"I mean, it'd be more 'I'm going to punch her lights out,'" he added.

Hana was satisfied.

"Yeah. She'd deserve it, but I think I'd much prefer just never seeing her again."

"Well, I think Rebecca's parents will be just as excited to see her," Mr Sim said.

Hana jumped. "Oh, sorry," She said. "I forgot you were here. How do you know them exactly?"

"My Aunty Jess was one of Rebecca's godparents. She and her fiancé – what was his name? Jared? I think it was Jared Choules. Anyway, they were looking after Rebecca when they were kidnapped. When the three of them didn't return, my parents became close with Rebecca's parents."

"Must have been hard for you all," Hana said. "I can't imagine something like that happening."

"I was 10 at the time," Mr Sim said. "My parents didn't talk about it much. But it obviously affected them, especially my dad. Rebecca's parents were devastated."

"Oh, that reminds me, we should call her Rebecca when we're down there," Aron said to Hana.

"Why do you keep calling her Penny, anyway? That's not her name," Mr Sim said.

"It's the only name we knew until recently. She's been on the ship with us every day for, what, five months?"

"Well, I think you should reconsider. Doesn't it bother Rebecca?"

"I don't mind at all," Penny called across. "I'm still getting used to being called 'Rebecca'. It doesn't sound natural coming from them, though."

"We told Penny-slash-Rebecca we'd call her whatever she wants us to call her," Aron said.

"If she is fine with it, that's ok. But definitely use her real name with her parents today."

"Absolutely."

There was a pause for a few moments as nobody had anything further to say on the matter.

"Ok, can I ask another question?" Mr Sim asked.

"Sure."

"Why didn't you bring Rebecca back as soon as you found her?"

Aron was suspicious. "Why do you ask?"

"Well, some of the officers at the station were talking about bringing charges against you. They argued that as you didn't immediately bring Rebecca back here, that suggested that you'd intended to keep her a slave but then changed your mind. I protested, of course. I managed to convince them that they'd have difficulty convincing a judge of your guilt given that you had freed her."

"No way! Aron was trying to free me as soon as he found out!" Penny exclaimed, walking over this time.

"But why not come back immediately?"

Aron shrugged. "We had a pre-booked job to Beadful that we couldn't afford to be late for. We could have brought her back after that, I suppose."

Mr Sim shook his head. "Belike that wouldn't have been enow. You would have needed to take her directly to the nearest checkpoint."

"But that would have cost me the job! I can't afford to lose jobs like that. It would have ruined me!" Aron protested.

"Oh, I get that; I'm just talking with my law-enforcement hat on."

"But a judge would consider that a mitigating factor, right?" Hana asked.

"Not as often as you might think. Besides, you would have been arrested and spent time behind bars at that point."

Aron had a look of disbelief. "So my choices were free Penny, go to jail, or lose my business?"

"The fact that she has vouched for you would probably mitigate things greatly. You would probably have only received a minimal amount of jail time."

The look on Aron's face told Mr Sim that wasn't a consolation.

"I know, it's not great. But it's set up this way for a reason. People exploit soft laws all the time."

Aron decided not to argue. He counted himself lucky to have managed to avoid legal trouble. Still, it angered him that it was because they had taken the matter into their own hands.

Penny looked sympathetic but decided to move on. "Which village do I come from?" She asked, turning to look out at the mountains.

"Swanbrook. You can't see it from here," Mr Sim said. "It's tucked in behind the south arm of the mountain over there. That's Swan Mountain. It's supposed to look like a sleeping swan, but I've never seen it."

"How big is Swanbrook?"

"About a thousand people. It's actually one of the larger settlements on Feng. Bonnie Hill is the largest settlement. That's right below us at the base of the creeper; it's got a population of ten thousand."

"Feng's such a small place! Especially given how close it is to everything. Especially given how much land it has!" Hana said.

"Land isn't everything, Hana," Aron teased.

"Most of it is owned by the forestry industry," Mr Sim said. "You can see their current work over that way."

Mr Sim pointed to a large patch of visible dirt north of Swan Mountain.

"Why do they need so much land?"

"Belike they don't. But they've owned it since Feng was founded. And there's not much demand for it. I hear they'd always looking to sell land if the price is right."

"We're getting close now," Penny exclaimed.

They could now see Bonnie Hill quite clearly. The causeway from the creeper led to a bridge across the mouth of a small harbour.

The town was divided by two perpendicular boulevards. Where the two met stood a rather ugly square clock tower. This was built with beige bricks, a concrete facade around the clocks, and a flat, mud-brown roof.

"It's such a pretty town!" Penny gushed.

"Clearly, you haven't seen our clock tower," Mr Sim said.

— — — — —

Once on ground level, they crossed the causeway and the bridge and then turned left towards Harbourside Park. There was a small rotunda between two trees in the middle of the park. Inside the rotunda, an older couple waited.

"That's Martin and Margaret; your parents, Rebecca," Mr Sim said. Then he turned aside and spoke to Aron and Hana quietly. "If you don't mind, I think it's best if I introduce Rebecca to her parents, and then we give them some time. We can wait back here until they're ready for us."

"Sure, that makes sense," Aron said, while Hana nodded beside him.

Mr Sim led Penny across the grass to the rotunda.

"What if that's not really her parents?" Hana suddenly asked. "What if Mr Sim is a mole?"

"I'm getting weird separation anxieties too. But Mr Sim is a mole? That's just paranoid."

Penny and Mr Sim reached the rotunda. There was a bit of chatting, a couple of teary hugs, and a bit more talking. Then all of a sudden, Penny started to look agitated. She grabbed the hand of the woman and, with the man and Mr Sim trailing, dragged her over to where Aron and Hana stood.

"These are the people who saved me!" Penny stated firmly.

"What's going on?" Hana asked.

"The police told my parents that they rescued me!"

"It might have been a miscommunication," Martin Maguire interjected.

"I don't care!" Penny said forcefully. "I want it clear that these two, and Aron's brother Marc, risked a lot to bring me back here. All the police did was make a phone call."

Margaret Maguire didn't look surprised or confused; she was just happy. "Thank you!" She said emphatically. Then she pulled Aron and Hana into a hug. Penny and her father quickly joined.

"Let's take Rebecca for a walk to get reacquainted," Martin said after the hug had run its course.

"I hope you two stick around. We'll treat you two to dinner tonight." Margaret said.

"That's not to suggest that bringing our daughter back is only worth a dinner," Martin pointed out. Margaret mouthed a horrified 'oh no!' at the thought.

"We'd love to," Hana said, with Aron nodding beside her.

Penny and her parents walked away.

"I'm sorry," Mr Sim said. "I don't know what the police told her parents, but they shouldn't have claimed credit."

"It doesn't matter. Penny will set the record straight." Aron said.

"Rebecca," Hana corrected.

— — — — —

Mr Sim had quickly left to make some calls. That left Aron and Hana waiting around for Penny to return. After an hour or so, they did.

Penny's mother had long prepared for this reunion. She had read that taking things slowly at the first meeting was good. So they agreed to separate again until dinner. This was easier said than done; many tears were shed at this parting.

Aron, Hana, and Penny decided to explore more of the town.

"How are you feeling?" Aron asked.

Penny was silent for a while as she tried to put it into words. Eventually, she gave up. "I can't explain it!" she said. "There's just so many different things that I feel!"

"But generally good, I hope."

Penny smiled. "Yes. Definitely. I feel like I already know them, somehow. I was a bit terrified at first; I didn't know what to expect. But they're just how I thought they would be."

"I'm so glad!" Hana said.

"We're both glad," Aron said.

"They're asking if I'd like to stay for a while."

"That'd be good." Hana nodded.

"I don't know. I've only just met them. I mean, they're my parents, but —"

"It'll be fine!" Hana assured her. "Anyway, we can probably stay nearby for a while, just in case."

"No problem there," Aron added. "I'm sure Feng has other sights to see. Maybe a second clock tower. Or a giant fish sculpture."

"They have an open-air museum," Hana said, missing the sarcasm.

"Ok. But will you guys stay there with me the first night?"

"Whatever you need, Penny," Aron said.

"Aron! It's Rebecca here!" Hana scolded him.

Penny just smiled and pulled them both in for a hug.

— — — — —

After dinner, Aron, Hana, and Penny headed back towards the creeper, having agreed to come and stay with Penny's parents the night.

"Have you thought about what you're going to do now?" Aron asked Penny. "I mean, long term."

"I'm going to stick around here for a while. Get reacquainted with my family. Apparently, I've got uncles, aunts, and cousins to meet," Penny said.

"What about for a career?"

"I'm still hoping I could come work with you. I can do your finances, and maybe I can learn to be a pilot, too," Penny said.

"What about your family?" Hana asked. "Wouldn't you prefer something nearby?"

"I don't want to sound calloused – I've just met them after all – but I can't just be here to be their kid. I've already grown up out there."

"You know this job doesn't pay very well," Hana said.

"It pays better than my last job." Penny laughed.

"Touché"

"Speaking of the future, what are *we* doing next?" Hana asked Aron.

"I have no idea. We're stuck here until we can find another trained pilot," Aron said. "Do you reckon Hahaha would come back if we asked?"

"Oh, sure! He'd be giving up a decently-paying job to work for basically nothing. Plus, he's getting married soon; but I'm sure they both can squeeze into a bunk on our tiny ship."

Aron rolled his eyes. "Sarcasm acknowledged."

"I'm sure we can find someone to fill in at least temporarily," Hana said.

"Sure," Aron said. "It will be difficult to organise a temporary pilot when we don't have definite cargo. And it'll be difficult to organise cargo without a full crew."

"Shouldn't be that hard, surely. That's the point of temp agencies."

Just then, Penny's phone rang. She stepped away to answer it.

"To be honest, I'm just glad this whole slave thing is over so things can go back to quiet and settled without having so much to worry about," Aron said.

"Definitely," Hana said. Then she leaned in and asked. "Who's calling her?"

"Belike it's her parents," Aron responded.

"We only just–"

"Aron, it's someone from the Angish Central News Service. They want to talk to you," Penny said, handing the phone to Aron.

"So much for things being quiet," Aron said, covering the mouthpiece as he took the phone from Penny.

"Well, at least you can't say it's boring!" Hana exclaimed.

Appendices

A brief guide to Tun

Letters, numbers, and punctuation:

⟨sym⟩	L	Lad	⟨sym⟩	R	Rot	⟨sym⟩	T	Time
⟨sym⟩	M	Mad	⟨sym⟩	B	Bet/vet	⟨sym⟩	D	Dime
⟨sym⟩	N	Need	⟨sym⟩	E	Net/aim	⟨sym⟩	A	Am
⟨sym⟩	S	Seed	⟨sym⟩	U	Luck/Luke	⟨sym⟩	K	Kind
⟨sym⟩	G	Got	⟨sym⟩	P	Pet	⟨sym⟩	H	Hind
⟨sym⟩	I	In	⟨sym⟩	F	Of	⟨sym⟩	O	Not

∂ becomes long at the end of words. Y varies between words.
The sound of ⅂ varies between regions.

⟨sym⟩	SP	⟨sym⟩	RS	⟨sym⟩	NK	⟨sym⟩	FR
⟨sym⟩	ST	⟨sym⟩	BL	⟨sym⟩	PL	⟨sym⟩	TR
⟨sym⟩	SK	⟨sym⟩	BR	⟨sym⟩	PS	⟨sym⟩	KL
⟨sym⟩	GL	⟨sym⟩	NS	⟨sym⟩	PR	⟨sym⟩	KS
⟨sym⟩	GR	⟨sym⟩	NT	⟨sym⟩	FL	⟨sym⟩	KR

⟨sym⟩	⟨sym⟩	⟨sym⟩	⟨sym⟩	⟨sym⟩	⟨sym⟩	⟨sym⟩	⟨sym⟩	⟨sym⟩	⟨sym⟩
0	1	2	3	4	5	6	7	8	9
⟨sym⟩	⟨sym⟩	⟨sym⟩	⟨sym⟩		–	.	⟨sym⟩	✗	⟨sym⟩
10	11	*12*	*13*		–	.	,	?	!

Common phrases:

ⱶ⸔ꓵ.	Kras.	Yes.
ꓨ⸔ᐞ.	Gat.	No.
ꓨ⸔⸓ꓱ.	Gralu.	Hello.
ᐞꓬꓮ ⸕ꓱꓵ ꓵꓬꓳ.	Sten tum sem.	Nice to meet you.
ꓵꓬꓳ ꓕꓬ⸗	Sem rid?	How are you?
ⱶꓮ ꓕꓬ⸗ ꓴꓬꓵ.	Kra rid pens.	I'm well.
ꓵꓬꓳ ꓕꓴⱶ⸗	Sem bak?	And you?
ꓨꓴⱶ.	Glad.	Thanks.
ꓨꓴⱶ ⱶꓬ⸕:	Glad krer!	Thank you very much!
⸕ꓱꓵ.	Pruns.	Don't mention it.
⸕ꓬꓨꓬⱷ ⱶꓮ.	Regrib kra.	Excuse me.
ⱶꓮ ꓕꓴꓵꓵ.	Kra bask.	I'm sorry.
ꓵꓬꓳ ꓸꓬꓯ ⸕ꓬꓕⱷꓲꓵⱷꓵ ꓸꓬⱶ⸗	Sem pers ribsusos pek?	Can you please repeat?
ꓵꓬꓳ ꓸꓬꓯ ꓳⱷ⸗ ꓸꓬⱶ⸗	Sem pers nut pek?	Can you please speak slower?
ꓵꓬꓳ ⱶꓕꓵꓲ ⱶꓮ ꓸꓬⱶ⸗	Sem kaks kra pek?	Can you please help me?
ⱶꓮ ⸕ꓬꓵꓵꓨᐞ.	Kra prink gat.	I do not understand.
ꓵꓬꓳ ꓸꓬꓯ ꓬꓳꓵꓵꓲⱷ⸗	Sem pers Englis?	Do you speak English?
ⱶꓮ ꓸꓬꓯ ꓨ⸔ᐞ ⸔ꓱꓱ.	Kra pers gat Tun.	I do not speak Tun.
ⱶꓮ ꓱꓸꓳ ꓨ⸔ᐞ ꓵꓬꓵ.	Kra flam gat spens.	I am lost.
ⱶꓮ ⱶꓬ⸕.	Kra klir.	I do not feel well.
ꓵꓬꓳ ⱶꓬꓲ ꓵꓬꓳꓨꓬꓵ⸗	Sem kles sembel?	What is your name?
ꓵꓬꓳ ꓵꓬꓳꓨꓬꓵ ⱷⱶⱷꓲ.	Sem sembel Aron.	My name is Aron.
ꓵꓬꓳ ⱶꓬꓲ ꓴꓬꓵ⸗	Sem kles braps?	Where are you from?
ꓵꓬꓳ ꓴꓬꓵ ⱷꓴⱷꓵꓲ.	Sem braps Angis.	I come from Angish.
ꓸꓬꓱ ⱶꓬꓲ ꓲꓬꓱ⸗	Pel kles siks?	How much does it cost?
ꓸꓬꓱ ꓵꓬꓱ ⸗ꓯꓸꓲ ꓲꓵ.	Pel siks draks 50.	It costs 60 Drax.
ⱶꓬꓲ ꓱꓸꓳ⸗	Kles bam?	What is the time?
ꓱꓸꓳ ⸕ ⸔ꓬꓵ ꓲꓴꓵ.	Bam 9 trenk hans.	It is 1 PM.
ⱶꓸꓵ ⱶꓸꓵꓱ:	Kant kantu!	Hope remains!

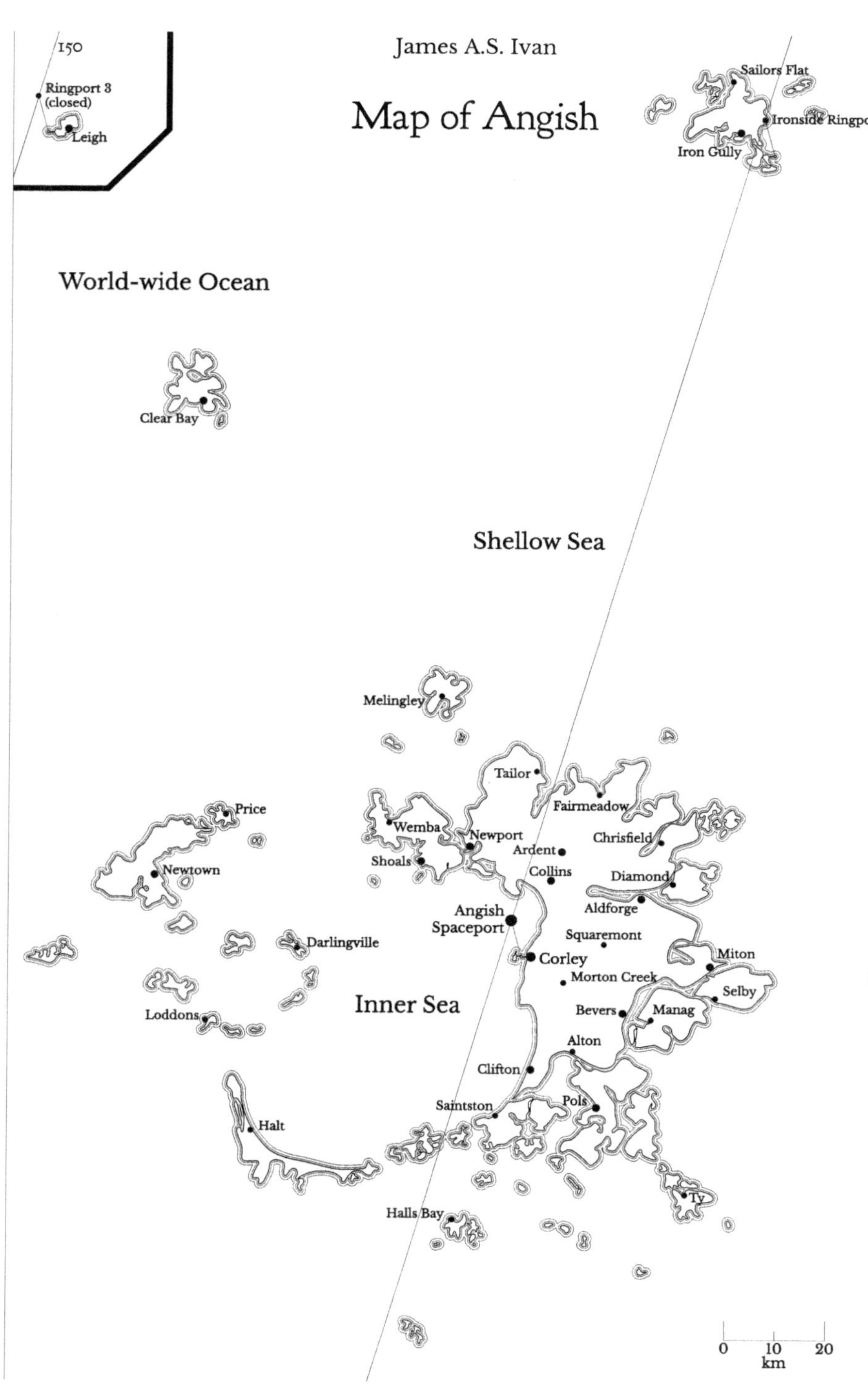

150
Ringport 3 (closed)
Leigh
James A.S. Ivan
Map of Angish
Sailors Flat
Ironside Ringport
Iron Gully
World-wide Ocean
Clear Bay
Shellow Sea
Melingley
Tailor
Fairmeadow
Price
Wemba
Newport
Chrisfield
Shoals
Ardent
Newtown
Collins
Diamond
Aldforge
Angish Spaceport
Squaremont
Darlingville
Miton
Corley
Morton Creek
Selby
Loddons
Inner Sea
Bevers
Manag
Alton
Clifton
Pols
Saintston
Halt
Ty
Halls Bay
0   10   20
km